BELONGING

In a tiny Yorkshire village, Harriet is lost in grief for Richard, her lover who died a year ago. His family blames her for the breakup of his marriage, but the truth is more complicated. Harriet has had no contact with them since Richard's death — until his daughter Niamh turns up on her doorstep one day, needing a sympathetic ear, followed by her uncle Tim. Tim is loyal to his sister, Richard's ex, but finds himself attracted to Harriet. Can the two of them overcome their differences and give in to love?

Books by Rhoda Baxter
in the Linford Romance Library:

GIRL ON THE RUN

RHODA BAXTER

BELONGING

Complete and Unabridged

LINFORD
Leicester

First published in Great Britain in 2018

First Linford Edition
published 2020

A catalogue record for this book is available from the British Library.

ISBN 978–1–4448–4514–3

Published by
Ulverscroft Limited
Anstey, Leicestershire

Set by Words & Graphics Ltd.
Anstey, Leicestershire
Printed and bound in Great Britain by
T. J. International Ltd., Padstow, Cornwall

This book is printed on acid-free paper

Dedication
To my family. Always.

1

It was so dark it felt like the middle of the night, and when Harriet slammed the taxi door, it sounded like a gunshot in the deserted village street. There would be curtains twitching in a minute. The only place with lights on was the bakery where Sue would be at work on her bread already. Sanctimonious cow. Sue had caught Harriet doing the walk of shame at four in the morning many a time and would always make some comment. Imagine what she'd have to say about her going out midweek.

Harriet stepped with exaggerated care up to the door at the side of her corner shop, two doors along the street from the bakery. Her feet were already numb in these stupid shoes and it wouldn't do to twist her ankle as well. Angling her body away from the street light so that she could see the keyhole, she had a couple of stabs before she got the key in the lock and stumbled in.

After the darkness outside, the light in the narrow hallway was blinding. She covered her eyes and peered through her fingers. The stairs seemed to pulse ahead of her. Urgh. Not good. The hangover was going to be brutal tomorrow . . . well, later today, technically. She had to open the shop in five hours.

She went up the stairs on her hands and knees, pausing at the top to take off her heels. There was another door at the top. Harriet unlocked that too, took a deep breath and pushed it open.

The flat was exactly as she'd left it. Fairly neat. Fairly tidy. Totally empty, apart from her. She chucked her shoes into the basket in the corner and padded to the kitchen, where she got herself a glass of water. Of course it was empty. What had she expected? That he would miraculously be there waiting for her? And what if he had? What would he have said to find her staggering home smelling of booze and smoke and some random guy she'd pulled in a nightclub?

Harriet gulped down another mouthful of cold water. He'd be horrified and upset, that's what. There would be tears and remorse and she'd feel awful. But she'd happily live through that . . . just to see him again for five minutes.

Oh balls. This was what she'd gone out to avoid. This . . . yearning. She didn't have any more booze in the house. There was wine downstairs, in the shop, but she had enough sanity left to know that was out of bounds. Tears leaked down her cold cheeks. Harriet wove her way to the bedroom and, still dressed, curled up under the duvet and gave in to the sadness until she fell asleep.

* * *

When the alarm went off four hours later, Harriet smacked it to snooze and

3

uncurled, slowly, so that she didn't shatter herself into pieces. Ow. Ow. There was a band of pain around her head. She hauled herself up until she was vaguely sitting up, found the water and ibuprofen she'd put out on the bedside cabinet before she went out, and gulped it down. She reset the alarm and sank back under the duvet. One snooze and she'd go downstairs. All she had to do was sort the papers.

* * *

Sitting at his computer, Tim stared at his inbox. 212 messages. How was that even possible? He'd wrestled it down to less than 20 before going home the night before. He rubbed his eyes and briefly considered deleting the whole lot, just to see what happened. But no. That would be irresponsible. One of his graduate students might have emailed him something that was actually impor-tant. At least he could get rid of all the university administrative emails telling him about scheduled computer system updates or road closures. He sighed and started to work through them, trying to prioritise the onslaught so that he didn't get buried in it.

His mobile phone rang. He pulled it out and looked at the caller ID. Mel. Crap. He looked at his inbox and considered ignoring the call. She would only call back. He'd already had three missed calls from her that morning. She was nothing if not persistent, his twin sister.

He sank into his chair before he answered it. This was not going to be easy. Discussions with Mel never were.

'There you are,' she said by way of greeting. 'I've been trying to get hold of you for days. Don't you ever answer your phone?'

'Hi, Mel. I'm fine, thanks. You?'

She clicked her tongue. 'I know you're fine, Tim. I friended you on Facebook, remember?'

Had she? Oh bugger. He'd forgotten about that. He'd only friended her so that he could keep up with what his niece Niamh was doing. Of course it meant that Mel could see what he was up to, too.

'Anyway,' said Mel, 'I'm calling because I need a huge favour.'

There it was. Straight to the point. Although, on reflection, it saved a lot of time not beating about the bush. 'I dunno, Mel, I'm really busy at the moment.'

'I know you are, Tim. I wouldn't have called you if it wasn't urgent.'

Tim sighed. Fair enough. She was pretty self-sufficient. She had a husband and friends to lean on, anyway. 'What do you want, Mel?'

There was a tiny pause. 'You know how Alex and I are going away on a retreat in Scotland in a week's time.'

'Yes . . . '

'And Niamh was going to her godmother's place while we were away.'

Tim closed his eyes and rubbed at the headache that was gathering on his forehead. He had a feeling he knew what was coming. 'Mel, I can't look after Niamh. I'm completely snowed under with work. I have deadlines coming out of my ears and there's a new cohort of students arriving in two weeks. I — '

'Oh, Tim, please? Niamh's god-mother has broken her leg and she can't manage Niamh on top of that.'

'What is there to manage with Niamh? She's fourteen. She only needs an adult to be around. She doesn't need spoon-feeding.'

'Exactly! You could keep an eye on her in the evenings and make sure she gets something to eat. She's ever such a nice girl, she'll be no bother. She'll be spending the day at holiday club anyway, so you don't need to worry about her during the day.'

'Mel . . . ' he said. But his heart wasn't in it. Mel would keep trying to persuade him and he didn't have the energy to argue with her. She always won. Besides, he liked Niamh. Scratch that, he loved Niamh. He had spent a lot of time with her when Mel split up with her first husband. For a time, he had lived in his sister's house, acting as in-house babysitter while Mel sorted out mortgages and lawyers and got shot of Niamh's father Richard. Tim and Niamh had become very close as a result. Later, he'd been there to keep Mel calm while Richard took Niamh away on his access days. He and Mel argued and bickered, but if she ever needed him, he would be there. He would never to say no to her. And they both knew it.

'Please, please, please. You'll get to hang out with Niamh without me around. I've asked everyone else I can think of. You're my last hope.'

'Oh thanks.' He leaned back in his chair. 'Can't you cancel your trip?'

'You know I can't. It's taken me so long to arrange this. You know how hard it would be to get Alex to take time off again.' There was a telltale wobble in her voice. He recognised the latent panic in it. He knew what it meant. Mel's second marriage had been slowly deteriorating — according to Mel. Alex worked too hard and his initial adoration had faded to something more mundane. Mel was feeling ignored ... and Mel hated being ignored. Tim had initially wondered if Mel was just being a drama queen, but he now knew that she was genuinely worried.

'Okay,' he said. 'I'll do it. I'll come and stay at yours, but I'll have to work in the evenings. Niamh will pretty much have to entertain herself.'

Mel gave a little laugh. 'She'll be fine with that. All she ever wants to do is sit on Skype to her friends or watch Netflix.'

Tim smiled. Teenagers. Then he remembered all that had happened in Niamh's life in the past few months. 'How is she?' he asked. 'Is she okay?'

Mel sighed. 'Yeah. She seems to be ... getting on with things. She still bursts into tears from time to time, but not so often now. Mostly, she worries about friends and hairstyles and the usual stuff now.'

'Oh good. And how about you?'

'Well, I'm not exactly upset about Richard dying,' she said too quickly. 'I've got enough to worry about keeping my marriage to Alex alive.'

Tim frowned. Despite her brusque manner, he could feel the worry that bubbled underneath. 'How's that going?'

Mel sighed. 'In all honesty, I don't know. A fortnight in a retreat, with no computers or mobiles, might get Alex away from his computer long enough to sort things out . . . or it might just prove that we can't be fixed. I don't know.'

For a few seconds there was silence. The years fell away and they were six again. Tim, with scrubbed clean hands and paper face mask, was sitting on Mel's hospital bed, playing Scrabble with the hospital's special set that smelled of disinfectant. He'd had a brilliant six-letter word all lined up, but one look at his sister sitting there with tubes coming out of her nose and wrist, and he'd ignored it in favour of a lousy three-letter one. He'd let her win then and had been letting her win ever since.

There was no point fighting it. It was just a waste of precious time. 'You go to your retreat,' Tim said quietly. 'I'll keep an eye on Niamh.'

'Thanks, Tim. You're . . . well, thank you.'

Tim laughed. 'The words you're looking for are 'you're awesome'.'

She clicked her tongue. 'Oh don't you start. You hardly inspire awe.' Her voice softened, as though she was about to laugh too. 'But yes, thank you.' A beat passed. 'Can you come round at about four on Friday? I'll run you through everything before I head off.' And just like that, they were back to business.

'Sure. I'll see you Friday.'

He was smiling when he hung up. He could take a bit of time off to hang out with his niece at the weekend. It had been weeks since he'd last seen her.

With a jolt, he realised it had actually been months. Time flew. He opened his email and looked at the five messages that had come in while he was on the phone. This mountain of work would still be there, whether he took the weekend off or not. Maybe some of it would even go away. Maybe doing something different wasn't such a bad idea.

2

Tim arrived at his sister's house half an hour later than expected. Mel waved his apology away with an impatient flick of her hand.

'There's food in the fridge,' she said. 'There's a Tesco order on Monday. We're not expecting anyone to call for anything, apart from the guys who are coming to repair the greenhouse. That's next week. It's all written on the calendar.' She swanned off up the stairs as she spoke, forcing Tim to hitch his laptop bag up and follow her. 'You're in the guest room,' she said. 'You know where everything is. I've sent you the list of what Niamh is allowed to do. She knows the rules.' She paused at the door of the guest room. 'In fact, where is she? Niamh? Niamh.'

While his sister was distracted, Tim ducked past her into the room and dumped his laptop bag onto the bed. His other bag was in the car. It could come in later. In the hallway, Mel barked, 'Niamh, get down here. NOW!'

Mel lived in the nice part of town, in a tidy four-bedroomed house that had a garden big enough to have a greenhouse in it. Unlike the flat that Tim rented, it felt airy and full of light. He leaned against the window frame and looked out at the well-tended front lawns in the street. One day, he would be able to live in a place like this. Although in all honesty, he spent all his time either at his laptop or crashed out in front of the telly these days, so what was the point of a nice house if you barely noticed it? Besides, this was the sort of place that needed more than one person to make it feel lived in. He'd had hopes that Sarah . . . He shook his head. No. He couldn't think about that. That way lay misery.

There was a hissed mother/daughter argument taking place on the stairs down from Niamh's attic room. Tim rubbed his eyes. This was not a great start.

Outside, a dark car pulled up. Mel's husband Alex got out. Alex was still in his suit and, by the time he reached the front door, on the phone again. Tim liked Alex. He worked too hard, according to Mel, but apart from that, seemed nice enough. He was kind to Niamh, which counted for a lot in Tim's opinion.

'Oh, thank goodness, Alex is here,' said Mel.

There was a clatter of footsteps and Mel and Niamh came downstairs. Right now, with matching expressions of annoyance, they looked exactly alike — both slim and blonde, with the same oval faces — like time-lapse images of each other. Niamh gave Tim a nod by way of a greeting before she got dragged downstairs by her mother. Tim followed.

'You're late,' Mel said to Alex. 'Now we're going to be late.'

Alex held up a finger. 'Yes, I'll be

back by then. Okay. Look, I've got to go,' he said into the phone. After a few seconds, he said 'Thanks' and hung up. 'I'm sorry,' he said, giving Mel a perfunctory kiss on the cheek. 'Things overran.'

'You're not going to be able to use that thing while you're on the retreat,' said Mel, pointing at the mobile phone. 'So you may as well leave it behind.'

Alex gave her an incredulous glare and put his phone in his pocket. 'Are you leaving yours?'

'No, but I've got to have it to check in on Niamh.' Mel strode into the living room, where the packed bags were waiting. 'There are the bags. Let's get going, or we won't get there until the small hours, and we're supposed to be in mindfulness class by nine tomorrow morning.'

'Can I at least get changed first?' said Alex.

'No! We're late already.' Mel was practically jumping with impatience.

Alex put a hand on her shoulder.

'How about you practise your breathing for a moment. Slow down. That's what this retreat is all about.'

'But — '

Alex strode past Niamh and Tim and disappeared upstairs. Tim caught Niamh's eye. Was it always like this? Niamh shrugged and looked away.

Mel clicked her tongue. 'You see what I mean?' she said to Tim.

Tim took another glance at Niamh, who had hunched into herself and was watching her mother through her hair. 'Tell you what,' he said. 'Why don't we put the bags in the car while we wait for Alex.'

'Good idea.' Mel grabbed her handbag. 'I have spare keys.' She pulled out the keys, picked up one of the bags, leaving Tim to pick up the other, and went outside.

Tim glanced at Niamh again, who rolled her eyes and picked up a smaller day bag. They took the bags outside and popped them in the boot of the car. Tim arranged the bags so that they wouldn't slide around too much on the drive.

He got back to the hallway just as Mel pulled Niamh to her in a fierce hug and kissed her forehead.

'Now be good and don't give Uncle Tim any trouble.' Mel patted her daughter on the cheek. Niamh rolled her eyes. Her eyes were the thing that was different from her mother's. Where Mel's eyes were blue, Niamh's were startling green, like her late father's.

Alex appeared on the stairs behind them. He had changed into jeans and a shirt, but he still looked distinguished, with his long clean-cut face and hair that was greying at the temples. Tim wasn't greying yet, but he was willing to bet money that he wouldn't do it as gracefully as Alex did.

'And you,' said Mel, pointing at Tim and making him jump. 'Look after my precious baby.'

'Muuum!' said Niamh.

'Well you are precious,' said Mel.

'And I will look after her. Or we'll

look after each other. Now you go off and enjoy yourself,' said Tim.

'I won't be able to have my phone on me most of the time, so you'll have to call the main reception if there's anything urgent. Have you got the number?'

'Yes,' said Tim. He stood next to his niece. 'We'll be fine. Won't we, Niamh?'

'Yeah. Bye, Mum. Have a great time. You too, Alex.' Niamh stood by the door, her back to Tim, and waved her mother and stepfather off. When at last the car pulled away, Niamh closed the door and turned to him. 'I don't know why Mum thought you needed to come,' she said. 'I don't need a babysitter.'

Tim put up his hands. 'Woah, steady on. You're fourteen. Mel can't leave you alone in the house for two weeks. Anyway, I'm not here to babysit. I have work to do. I'm just here to be an adult presence if you need one. Okay?'

Niamh stuck her hands in her jeans pockets and looked at him through her hair. 'What does that mean?'

'I don't know,' said Tim. 'Your mum left me a list of rules . . . Look, I need a coffee. Let's go see what she's said and figure out what we can live with.'

By the time they'd made coffee, the atmosphere was a little lighter. Niamh even cracked a smile.

'Oh come on,' said Tim. 'It's not that bad having your uncle to hang out with.' She used to adore him.

Niamh didn't say anything, but she pulled a face. 'At least you'll be better than Mum and Alex.'

Tim raised an eyebrow. As a child, Niamh had been really impressed by that. Clearly, now that she was older, being the cool uncle was a lot harder work.

'They need this retreat,' said Niamh meaningfully. 'Things were getting . . . snappy.'

Oh dear. No wonder Mel had been so adamant about going. With one failed marriage behind her, she would be keen to keep this one intact. If

Niamh had noticed, then things must have deteriorated further than Mel had let on. 'Ah. That bad, huh?'

'Yeah. Things aren't the best around here at the moment.'

He looked at her for a second. The attitude had subsided a little. Enough to let him see that she looked tired and worried. Poor kid. It had been a tough year for her. First her father's sudden death, now this. 'How are you, Niamh? Are you okay?'

'Well, I could be better,' said Niamh. She fiddled with her nails, picking off nail varnish. 'Uncle Tim? Could you do me a favour?'

Uh oh. He knew that tone. It was almost exactly the same tone that Mel used before she bossed him into doing something. 'Depends what it is,' he said cautiously.

'Could you take me to Yorkshire?'

He laughed. He hadn't been expecting that. 'Whatever for?'

'I want to go see Harriet.'

A prickle of alarm shot down his

back. 'Who's Harriet?' he asked, even though he knew exactly who Harriet was. She was the woman who had wrecked Mel's first marriage. Richard's mistress.

'Dad's girlfriend.' She kept picking at her nails, not looking up.

He had only met the Harriet woman once, at Richard's funeral, when she'd stood, a silent, drooping figure, not speaking to anyone. But then, why would she? The rest of the people there were Richard's friends and family and it appeared he'd never introduced her to any of them.

'Why do you want to go see her?'

'I just do, okay? Will you take me?' Finally she looked up, eyes flashing.

'No. Well, I can, but I'd have to ask your mother first.'

Niamh shot to her feet. 'No. She never — ' She made an 'ugh' noise. 'Never mind.' She stamped off.

Tim listened to her footsteps thumping up the stairs and drank his coffee. That could have gone better.

3

Harriet staggered down the narrow stairs. She still felt nauseous after another mad Friday night, but her head had stopped pounding and the lag between her turning her head and her vision catching up was gone, which meant she could go down and get the stocktake sorted out.

Ash was behind the till, leaning on his elbows and reading a paperback. On Saturday mornings, he arrived at eight, delivered the papers and took over from Harriet by eight thirty. She had gone back to bed after he'd arrived.

He was a slim-hipped kid with dark chocolate skin and a smattering of acne. He read all the time. As far as Harriet could tell, there was no pattern to it; he read everything. It was weird. He looked up as she came in through the connecting door. 'Afternoon,' he said pointedly.

She was late. She knew that. Only about half an hour, but still, when you lived above your place of work, it was awkward. She waved a hand. 'I'll make it up. I'm only on for four hours today.'

Ash shrugged. 'Were you out again last night, then?'

'Uhuh.' She grabbed a coffee from the pot in the back room and found the stock lists that she'd printed out the evening before.

'Where'd you go?'

She told him the name of the nightclub.

'Oh yeah,' he said. 'I've been there.'

'Have you?' She'd never heard him mention going clubbing. She'd assumed he just stayed at home and read.

He shrugged. 'It was all right. Not really my scene, to be honest. All that clubbing and drinking. Waste of money. I'd rather go to the pictures or something. At least you get to be entertained and not feel like crap the next morning.' He raised an eyebrow at her, or tried to. The smile ruined the judgemental look

24

he was going for.

'Shut up,' she retorted. 'Cheeky git.' She shuffled into the stockroom and started at the far end. After a few minutes, she called out, 'Has it been busy today, then?'

'Not really,' Ash called back. 'The usual Saturday-morning regulars. Oh, the pub called to say that we need to deliver the *Sunday Times* and the *Independent* tomorrow as well as the usual haul. They've got people staying.'

The pub tended to take the *Yorkshire Post* and the *Courier* as standard. They only got the rest of the papers in if guests requested them. 'Have you — '

'It's in the order book,' he interrupted. The chime on the door rang, signalling a customer. Harriet went back to her work.

★ ★ ★

When it was time for a break, Harriet took her third coffee with her to let Ash off for a few minutes. He grinned at her and put a bookmark into his book.

'What're you reading now?' she asked.

He held it up for her. Sci-fi/fantasy. It was Jane Austen and some sort of thriller last week. She shook her head. 'You read the weirdest collection of stuff.'

'It's a big world,' said Ash. 'You've got to see it from lots of different angles.' He slipped off the stool he'd been sitting on.

'I've done my seeing the world.' Harriet plonked her coffee down and clambered onto the still-warm stool.

Ash stopped. 'Really? When?'

'One summer I did a really lucrative project. When the money came in, I went Interrailing.' She smiled. 'Met a great guy en route.'

She could see him hesitating, wondering if that was Richard. His lips moved, as though he had words lining up, but he didn't ask. She was clearly alone now. It was nice of him to show that much sensitivity.

'You can ask,' she said. 'It was just a

summer thing. We stayed in touch for a bit after we got back, but it wasn't meant to be. He lives in the US now. Married, with a couple of kids.'

She knew the question in his expression wasn't about that. He wanted to know why she was alone *now*. She hadn't told anyone in the village about Richard, just let them assume he'd split up with her. It was better than the truth. Less painful. Of course, everyone wanted more information, gossip, but she wasn't going to give any of them a chance to ask her that. She turned away. Thankfully, a customer came in.

★　★　★

A reminder went off on Tim's phone. While he was keeping an eye on Niamh, he tried to get 'home' to Mel's house before Niamh was dropped off after holiday club, which meant leaving at four thirty. He sighed and turned the reminder off. He'd tried to plan his day so that the paperwork that needed review was left until the end. He could take that home. It was Friday now, and he and Niamh had fallen into a companionable pattern where they sat with their respective laptops in separate rooms until it was time for supper, when they ate together. She was a nice kid, a bit quiet and monosyllabic compared to how she used to be, but that was probably a teen thing. She was meant to be going to a friend's house after holiday club that day, so he could stay a little longer, but he had to go and pick her up from her friend's at a reasonable hour.

He stuffed the paperwork into a folder and put that and his laptop in the bag. Before he could log off, his phone rang.

'Hi, this is Faisal from the funding office. I've got a few queries about the grant application we were discussing earlier.'

'I'm about to leave. Can this wait until Monday?'

'Not really. There's a six-day review

period, and the deadline is — '

'Okay, fine. I've got a few minutes; what's the problem?' He sank back down and pulled up the relevant document.

It took another hour to get it resolved. He texted Niamh to say he was going to be late. A text arrived back saying, 'Don't worry about me. I'm fine. Niamh.' He read it and thought nothing of it.

★   ★   ★

Harriet finished off her work, diligently staying on an extra fifteen minutes to make sure everything was tidied up properly, ready for the next day. She always did. Mr Petovski trusted her, so she had to maintain that trust. He had done a favour by offering her part-time work in the shop when she'd fallen on hard times. She would not repay his kindness by slacking off.

After locking up the shop, she scooped up some of the stock that was to be written off because it had passed its use-by date, and headed up the stairs. The shop stocked a random assortment of things that people in the village might need in between their weekly trip to town for 'the big shop'. Apart from staples like bread, milk, cheese and wine, they also sold a variety of tinned items, eggs from a nearby farm, and a few cakes from the bakery.

In her flat, the phone was ringing. She carried a mobile phone out of habit, but rarely bothered with it when she was out of WiFi range, because the signal was so bad in the village. If you wanted to get a decent signal, you had to climb Hadly Top, and she'd stopped bothering years ago. A good old-fashioned landline and broadband did the job just as well.

She put the clutch of tins on the floor while she fished her keys out of her pocket. Who could be calling her? The only person who used to call at this hour was Richard. He'd phone her from Leeds to say he was on the train, which gave her just over 25 minutes to get over to Huddersfield station to pick him up. Since the accident, no one called. It was probably some insurance claims service asking if she'd had an accident at work again.

The phone stopped before she got in. The answerphone was flashing. She eyed it wearily. It was unlikely to be important. It was even less likely to be welcome news. She dumped the tins on the counter in the kitchen and sighed. Best check it out anyway. Maybe it was a copywriting client. She hadn't had any client work in months.

There were four messages. Odd. She pressed the button to hear them.

The first one was from that morning. 'Uh . . . hi . . . Harriet. It's Niamh. Um . . . you knew my Dad, Richard Howell and . . . Well, I didn't get to talk to you at the funeral, but I really need to talk to someone about Dad, and you're the only one I can think of. I hope you don't mind, but I'm coming up to see you. Please can you call me back on . . . '

Harriet stared at the machine, not

bothering to write down the number. Niamh. Richard's daughter Niamh. She had met her before, a sweet, shy girl with Richard's eyes. He had brought her up to the village once, when his ex-wife was out of the country. That was when Harriet had realised that Richard was genuinely serious about her. She had liked Niamh, but didn't really know her. She certainly didn't want to talk to her about Richard. She didn't want to talk to anyone about Richard. She hit delete.

The next message was Niamh again. 'I really hope this is still your number. Dad said you didn't have a mobile. He gave me this number in case I needed to get hold of him when he was up there with you and . . . well, anyway. I've just gone past Birmingham New Street and I'm on my way. I really hope you get this message. Please call me back.'

Niamh sounded slightly worried in this one. Harriet wondered what her mother was thinking, letting a fourteen-year-old travel up to Yorkshire by herself.

Unless Mel was with her daughter. Harriet shuddered. She'd only ever seen Mel once, at the funeral, and they were clearly not going to be friends.

The third message was similar to the second, only Niamh was starting to sound frightened. So, not with her mother then. Harriet frowned. What was going on? She skipped on to the last message. The one left a few minutes before.

'It's Niamh. Niamh Howell. Please, please call me. I'm on the train to Huddersfield and . . . oh God, I really hope you get this and come to meet me. I don't know your address or anything. I . . . I'll try and get a taxi to the village. I'm . . . please call. Please.'

The fear in the child's voice went straight through her. Harriet swore. She called the number back. It was engaged and went to answerphone. 'This is Harriet. Stay where you are. I'm coming.'

She picked up her car keys and left the flat.

4

Tim glanced at the clock on his computer. Yikes. He wasn't going to get back in time. He pulled up the photo he'd taken of Mel's note and copied down the number and address for the woman whose house Niamh was spending the evening at. He was supposed to pick her up twenty minutes ago.

'Hello, is that Wendy's mum?' he said when she picked up. 'This is Niamh's uncle, Tim. I'm just calling to say I'm running a little late, but I'm on my way to get her now.'

There was a pause at the other end. 'Niamh? . . . Niamh Howell?'

Unease prickled. Something was wrong. Was Niamh hurt? 'Is everything okay?'

'Um . . . you said she wasn't well and staying at home with you today . . . '

'What? No. I never called you before. I . . . I dropped her off outside holiday club this morning. I watched her go in the door!'

'No . . . you definitely called me this morning.' The woman's voice was starting to climb in pitch. 'She wasn't at holiday club, otherwise I would have picked her up when I got Wendy.'

Tim froze. Liquid panic replaced the blood in his veins. 'But where is she, then?'

'Hang on,' said the woman. 'I'm going to see if Wendy knows anything. I'll call you back.' She was already bellowing 'Wendy' when she put the phone down.

Shit. Shit. Shit. Where was Niamh? She'd been missing since the morning. What could have happened to her? He had definitely watched her go in through the door at the church hall where the holiday club was held. What could have happened between her entering, and her being signed in?

Breathe, Tim. Breathe. He should call the police. No. First he should try her phone.

He pulled up her number. It rang. And rang. *Come on come on come on. Answer.*

Finally, just when he was certain it was going to go to messages, she picked up. 'Where are you?' he demanded. 'I thought you were at Wend — '

A sob from Niamh sliced through his train of thought. 'Niamh? Where are you? Are you safe?'

Another sob, then, 'I'm such an idiot.'

'Where are you? I'll come and get you.' He stood up, ready to run out.

'I'm in . . . ' She sobbed. ' . . . York-shire. I've done something really stupid.'

'What — ' He bit off the words *have you done* just in time. 'What happened?'

'I needed to talk to someone about Dad. Mum won't talk about him, and there's no one else, and I miss him so much,' Niamh wailed. 'Harriet's the only one there is, and she's not answering her phone!'

'Wh — ?'

But Niamh wasn't finished. 'I thought

if I came up here, she could come and pick me up from the station like she did when Dad came up and . . . and . . . and she's not picking up her phone! She might even have moved since . . . Oh God, I'm such an idiot.'

Tim tried to unscramble what was going on and failed. Whatever it was, he needed to find his niece and make sure she was safe. Everything else could be ironed out later.

'Niamh,' he said, trying to project calm down the line. 'Niamh, tell me where you are. I'll come and get you.'

'I'm in Huddersfield.'

'What the fu — ' That was two hundred miles away. It would take him at least three hours to get there. In the meantime, she was alone, in the dark, in Yorkshire.

'I'm sorry! I thought that . . . didn't think that Harriet might not . . . oh, Uncle Tim. Mum is going to KILL me.'

Tim took a deep breath and let it out. His fingers flew over his keyboard as he got up Google maps. 'Okay. Okay.

Stay calm, Niamh. I'm going to come up and get you, but it's going to take me a while to get there. In the meantime, we need to get you somewhere safe where you can wait, okay? Let me think.'

★ ★ ★

It was dark by the time Harriet reached the station. After a few circuits, she found a parking space and jumped out. She still wasn't sure what she felt about this — annoyed, sad, apprehensive? All she knew was that she didn't want to see Richard's daughter. But the child was stuck in a railway station, in a town she didn't know, after dark. She had no option but to go find her.

The station glowed yellow-orange in the street light and gathering mist. It was almost spring, but it was still damp and chilly. Harriet pulled up the zip on her fleece as she hurried in. Inside the building, the light was harsh. There were a few people sitting or standing in the main entryway. It wasn't a big space. There were a few counters, all but one closed, a couple of tatty plastic seats, the steps into the underpass that led to Platforms 2 and 3, and big doors letting in the cold air from Platform 1.

Harriet looked around, trying to remember what Niamh looked like. A girl was sitting hunched over her backpack, which was on her lap, speaking to someone on the phone. Her face was hidden by her hair. Harriet took a step towards her.

The girl looked up. Harriet stopped as though she'd been stung. Those eyes. Richard's eyes. She had dreamt of seeing them again. She would have given anything to look into them again, just once. And now she was looking at them, set in someone else's face. Her insides contracted. No. She couldn't do this. She couldn't bear it.

The girl broke into a smile so full of relief that Harriet's heart flipped. Richard's daughter needed her. How could she turn her back on that?

Niamh said, 'She's here. It's okay,' into the phone and hung up. She wiped her hand across her cheeks and stood up. 'You came. Thank you so much,' she said.

Harriet couldn't speak, so she inclined her head.

Niamh's smile faltered. 'I . . . ' For a minute, she looked like she was about to cry again.

Harriet felt her own eyes fill up. Oh, Richard. He had adored his daughter. No matter how he and his ex-wife felt about each other, he had never stopped loving Niamh. Harriet cleared her throat. 'Are you okay?'

Niamh nodded. 'Yes. I'm . . . well, a bit cold, but otherwise . . . ' Her phone rang. She flicked it off without even looking at it. 'Thank you. For coming to get me. I . . . I guess I should have called and checked with you before I . . . uh . . . '

'Yes, you should have,' said Harriet. 'Well, you're here now. What were you planning to do?'

Niamh opened her mouth. Then shut it again. Clearly, she had no idea what she wanted to do. A stab of irritation pierced the heaviness in Harriet's chest. Niamh had just turned up, assuming Harriet would take care of her. Which was the height of cheek. But Niamh didn't look cocky right now. She looked cold and tired and scared.

'Does your mother know where you are?' Harriet demanded.

There was a 'clack' behind her. The man at the ticket desk rapped on the partition. 'Everything all right?' he said, leaning forward to look at them.

Oh heck. The last thing she needed was to be accused of abducting a teenager. 'We're okay,' said Harriet over her shoulder. She turned back to Niamh and said quietly, 'Niamh, does your mother know you're here?'

Niamh shook her head.

'She'll be frantic. You have to call her.'

'She's on a retreat with Alex.'

'And she left you alone?' Dear God.

41

'Oh, no. Uncle Tim's supposed to be looking after me.' She looked down at her feet. 'He didn't know I was coming here. I ran away.'

'You ran — ' Oh bloody hell. 'Call him,' said Harriet. 'Call him now and tell him where you are.'

'I told him. He knows I'm in Huddersfield. When you didn't answer the phone, I thought maybe I'd made a terrible mistake and — '

'You have,' said Harriet. 'You *have* made a terrible mistake.' She looked over her shoulder. The man behind the glass was watching them. She sighed. 'Look, since you're here and it's late, you'd better come with me.'

Niamh's face lit up with relief. 'Oh. Thank you!'

'But before we go anywhere, I want to talk to your Uncle Tim.'

Her face fell, but she didn't argue. 'Okay.' She pulled her phone out and called a number.

Harriet came and leaned against the wall next to Niamh, so that the man

42

behind the counter could see her clearly. From Niamh's phone came a stream of tinny babble as the man at the other end spoke.

'It's okay, Uncle Tim. Harriet's here now. Here, she wants to talk to you.' Niamh passed the phone across.

'Niamh, what the — ' the man said before Harriet cut him off with, 'Hello, this is Harriet Brown.'

There was a sharp intake of breath. A pause and then he said, 'I'm Tim Knowles. I'm Niamh's uncle. Er . . . her mother's brother.'

'Right,' said Harriet. 'Well, Tim, Niamh is here in Yorkshire, at a railway station. If she was in your care, where did you think she was?'

Another pause. Irresponsible man. He was probably trying to think of an excuse.

'I thought she was at holiday club. I dropped her off there this morning and . . . oh shit. Look, Harriet. I'm really sorry about this. I'm heading up to Yorkshire now. If you give me your address, or a place to meet, I'll come and get Niamh. It's about four hours' drive from here and — '

Harriet glanced at Niamh, who was staring up at her hopefully. She sighed. 'I'll take her to my flat,' she said. 'Have you got pen and paper? I'll give you my address.'

She could almost hear the cogs turning in the man's head. 'Really, Tim. You're all the way down south. And I'm here. My place is probably safer for Niamh than the train station.'

A sigh. 'Yes, yes. I'm sorry. Right. I've got pen and paper.'

She gave him her address and landline number. She also gave him the number for the pub. 'I have no food in the house,' she said. 'I'll take her to the pub in Trewton Royd and buy her some tea.' She thought of the out-of-date tins of soup. She couldn't risk the child getting food poisoning. 'The pub is called The Trewton Arms. It's across the road from my place. Okay?'

'Yes. Yes. Thank you. It's very kind of

you,' said Tim. 'I'll be there in a few hours.'

'Drive safely,' she said. She handed the phone back to Niamh and looked away. 'I'll be there in a few hours,' were the last words Richard had said to her. All it had taken was one lorry and a wet patch on the road. He hadn't even been on the motorway.

Niamh listened to her phone in silence for a few seconds and said, 'Yes, Uncle Tim. Okay, Uncle Tim. Bye.' She hung up and made a face. 'He's really pissed with me.'

Harriet glanced sideways at her and said nothing. 'Come on,' she said. 'Let's get you somewhere warm.'

In the car, they drove in silence for a few minutes. Harriet tried not to scowl as she drove out of the town and up the narrow roads that headed out to Trewton Royd. What was she meant to do with Niamh until this Tim fellow came to get her? She tried to remember some of the things Richard had said about Niamh. Rosy descriptions from a proud daddy. He would hardly have imagined his girl as someone foolish enough to run away.

After a while, Niamh said, 'Harriet?'

'Mmm?'

'Are you angry with me? I know I should have checked with you before I came, but Dad always said you had the biggest heart of anyone he'd ever met.'

He'd said that? Harriet cast a sideways glance at the girl in the seat next to her. The last time she'd seen her, she'd been about twelve. Not quite a teenager, not quite a little girl. She had been giddy with excitement meeting her father's girlfriend — this had baffled Harriet at the time, but Richard had explained that Niamh and her mother didn't always get on and that if Mel hated Harriet, Niamh would be predisposed to like her. Perhaps this was an extension of that.

'He said . . . ' Niamh's voice caught mid-sentence. ' . . . he said that there was nothing he couldn't tell you and that you always made him feel like he'd come home. And I thought . . . I'm sorry. I shouldn't have come.'

Harriet took a deep breath. 'Well, it's not so much that. You should have given me a bit of warning. And not running away would have helped.'

Niamh sniffed.

They crested the hill and descended into Trewton Royd. The village was at the bottom of the valley, a pool of light in the acres of darkness. Living above the shop meant that Harriet was right in the middle of the main street. She was also a few hundred yards from the pub, so they left the car parked outside the flat and walked across to the Trewton Arms.

Mentally thanking Mr Petovski for being a reliable boss who paid exactly on time, Harriet ushered Niamh into the pub. The Trewton Arms was an old-fashioned place with softly lit booths by the window. At the far end, a small fire danced, with a couple of armchairs pulled up to it. The regulars rarely bothered with the armchairs, but

47

people who came up for the weekend seemed to love them.

The regulars, perched on stools at the bar, turned to see who it was. Seeing it was Harriet, everyone returned to their drinks and conversations. Harriet ushered Niamh towards an empty table by a window.

The landlady, Angie, who was gathering glasses, stopped. 'Hello, Harriet. Don't often see you in.' She was speaking to Harriet, but her gaze was on Niamh. 'Hiya, love. You're a friend of Harriet's, are you?'

'This is Niamh. She's not had anything to eat since lunchtime; could we order some food?' Harriet jumped in before Angie started nosing around too much. She liked Angie, but bloody hell, that woman could gossip.

As predicted, the chance to feed a hungry child trumped curiosity. 'Oh, you poor love, you must be starving.' Angie patted Niamh's arm. 'What can I get you? We've got jacket potatoes and chilli. Or there's a burger and chips.'

'Burger, please,' said Niamh.

'I'll have the same,' said Harriet. 'Thank you so much.'

Angie turned, then paused. 'You'll be wanting a drink as well. I may as well get that for you at the same time.' She glanced at Harriet.

'We'll have two glasses of Coke, please. Pints,' Harriet said. She would normally have had a glass of wine, but right now she didn't trust herself to stop at one.

'Diet Coke,' said Niamh. 'Please.' She sat down and shrugged off her coat. She'd left her bag in the car. 'Thank you,' she said to Harriet. 'I'm really sorry that I didn't think this through.'

Harriet balled up her coat and threw it onto the seat. 'It's okay. Well, you're here now, so what did you want to talk to me about?'

Niamh stared at her hands for a moment. 'I . . . I'm not sure.'

Harriet waited and concentrated on her own breathing. If it wasn't something specific, this was even weirder than it appeared. Much as she loved Richard, she had never had any illusions that she was ever going to be Niamh's stepmother. It just wasn't something they'd wanted. Richard loved Niamh. Adored her. Mel . . . was an unfortunate hassle that came with access to Niamh. Mel would never allow Niamh to spend significant time with Richard and Harriet.

The silence stretched. Angie returned with their drinks. She looked like she was about to start chatting, but Harriet forestalled her with a tiny shake of the head. She indicated Niamh with her eyes. Angie got the message and returned to the bar, where she continued to throw curious glances across at them.

'I miss him,' said Niamh suddenly. She sniffed. 'I mean, it's not like we lived in the same house or anything, but I . . . I got to see him a lot and I miss him. It's like sometimes I think 'oh, I'll go hang out with Dad today' and then I remember.'

'And it's like you're feeling it for the

first time.' The words came out in a whisper. She knew that feeling all too well. That moment of disorientation before the knowledge slammed into you. When you forgot that he was no longer there. When you were, however briefly, content with life . . . and then you remembered. That explosion of grief that was every bit as painful as the first time. All the denial, the grieving, the getting past things, all undone in a single moment. Harriet had known it would be like that, but poor Niamh would have been caught unawares.

'Yes.' Niamh's eyes rose to meet hers. 'It hurts. Thinking about him hurts, but I want to think about him. I want to talk about him. I'm frightened that if I don't, I'll forget him.'

Harriet reached across and put her hand over Niamh's. The teenager looked up at her with Richard's eyes. Understanding passed between them.

'But why me?' Harriet said. 'I'm just the long-distance girlfriend. I only saw him every three or four weeks. I know he had a whole other life that I wasn't a part of. You know all of those people. Why do you want to talk to me?'

'Mum . . . well, you know what she's like. She doesn't want to have anything to do with Nan or any of Dad's friends. She tries hard to hide it, but she's still really angry with him about . . . well about you.'

Harriet opened her mouth to speak.

Niamh held up a hand. 'I know you didn't split my parents up. Dad said he met you after he and Mum split up, but Mum was having none of that.' She sighed. 'She refused to hear his name in the house for, like, months. Once she met Alex, she chilled a bit, but . . . ' She frowned and fiddled with the straw in her Coke, stirring the ice cubes round. 'The thing is, Mum and Alex aren't doing so well at the moment. So she's kind of preoccupied with that.'

'But your father died,' said Harriet. 'That's a big deal.' How could that woman not realise the effect that would have on her daughter?

'I know, right?' said Niamh. 'For the first few months she was all, like, cuddly and stuff. But then, after a while, you could tell she didn't want to talk about it. Or about Dad. She booked me in to have a chat with a therapist. But, well, it's not the same talking to a stranger, is it?'

Technically, she was still talking to a stranger. Harriet decided it was probably best not to mention that. Everything she knew about Niamh, she knew second-hand, filtered through the eyes of a father who adored his little girl. It seemed that Niamh's view of Harriet was similarly filtered through Richard.

'You loved him, you see,' Niamh continued. 'I just wanted to talk to someone who loved him. Someone who could tell me happy stuff about him. So that I can keep hold of all those good memories.'

Harriet nodded slowly. She could understand that. Poor Niamh. 'Okay. I see what you mean.' She rested her chin on her hands. 'Well, what did you want to know?'

Niamh's face lit up. 'Anything. Fun stuff. Like . . . how did you meet?'

'You know that story.'

'Tell me anyway. How come you were here in the first place?' She looked eager, almost desperate, like a child begging for a bedtime story to stave off nightmares. In a way, that was exactly what she was.

Harriet smiled. 'I had just been made redundant from the company I'd been working for. I was really unhappy there, so it was probably not the worst thing that could have happened. Anyway, I grew up in a village over that way.' She gestured through the window at the black hills in the distance. 'I thought I'd come back up to the area. I was I looking for a place to rent and I got here early. I took one look at Trewton Royd and it felt . . . right somehow. Like I belonged here.' She shook her head, smiling at the memory. 'I saw that the flat above the shop had a 'to let' sign outside, so on an impulse I went in to ask about it . . . and your dad was in the shop. There was some sort of discussion going on between the shop-keeper and another customer, so we got chatting. Afterwards, we went for a coffee together in the bakery and, well, the rest is history, as they say.'

Niamh dunked a chip in ketchup. 'What was Dad doing here?'

'He was renting a holiday cottage for a few days.' Getting away from Mel, he'd said. He was getting divorced and needed some space to think about what he was likely to have to lose in order to keep regular access to Niamh. 'The same place you stayed in when you were last here.'

'Oh yeah. I think he told me that.' Niamh's gaze was far away. 'When I came up with Dad that time, we went to see the Bronte Parsonage, do you remember?'

She remembered all right. They had looked round the parsonage and then gone into Haworth for tea and cake. Niamh had skipped on ahead. Harriet and Richard had followed, hand in hand, smiling indulgently. It was almost as though they were a family. She had been nervous about meeting Niamh, but she had turned out to be a lovely girl.

'I really wanted you to like me,' said Niamh. 'I was, like, on my best behaviour.'

At the time, Harriet had congratulated herself on getting on well with Richard's daughter. Now, she realised that the bright smiles and giggles hadn't been about her at all. They had been about Richard. Niamh knew her father wanted her to be happy to meet his girlfriend . . . so she was happy. Harriet's likeability was largely irrelevant. Getting On With Niamh had been such a big thing for her. She watched Niamh now, who have moved on to talking about something else from that weekend, and felt as though she'd had an award taken away.

Harriet looked down at her burger. She was no longer hungry. She put her cutlery down and rested her chin on her hand. 'What was he like?' she asked. 'At home, when you went to his for the weekend?'

Niamh blinked. 'Well, he was always busy, you know, with work and stuff. But when I stayed over, he'd turn his laptop off and we'd go out for the day. Before, when things were . . . you know, when he lived with me and Mum, I rarely saw him at the weekends. I kinda tagged around behind Mum all the time. And then, when they got divorced, suddenly he was there for me. How odd is that?'

Not odd at all. 'Were you upset? When your parents split up?' She hadn't really thought about that, because Niamh had seemed so balanced and happy when she'd met her. But what if she wasn't? What if that too was all an act to please Richard?

Niamh looked down. 'A bit,' she said. She traced a pattern on her plate in ketchup. 'Well, a lot, actually. Not so much when they finally decided to separate, but before that. They used to argue.

57

After I'd gone to bed. They'd try to keep it down, but I could hear them. You know, not the words . . . but the tone. It was . . . ' She shrugged. 'Not nice.'

'I'm sorry to hear that.'

'It's okay. It's not like it's your fault. They made each other unhappy. Mum . . . oh my God, Mum's like the total control freak. She needs to be right. All. The. Time. It drove Dad insane. It drives me insane too, but, you know, I can't divorce her. Looks like she's getting to Alex too.' Another shrug. 'Dad met you pretty soon after and he was happy.' She finally looked up. Green eyes. So familiar, yet not the same. 'You made him happy.'

The wave of emotion caught Harriet unawares. She wanted to say 'he made me happy too', but she couldn't speak. Her eyes filled with tears.

As if in response, Niamh gave a sob. 'I miss him.' A tear ran down her cheek and fell onto the plate. 'I miss him so much.' And she was crying quietly into her hands.

'Oh. Oh, honey.' Harriet shifted across and put an arm around the sobbing girl. She tried to say 'it's okay', but her own tears got in the way. Niamh turned and buried her face in Harriet's shoulder. Harriet put her arms around her and they held each other. Grieving for the man they both loved.

Looking up, Harriet saw Angie staring at her from behind the bar. Angie mouthed 'all right?' Harriet nodded over Niamh's head and her arms tightened protectively around the girl. They couldn't stay here. There was too much chance of awkward questions.

Niamh's sobs were easing off. Harriet loosened her hold and rubbed the tears off her own cheeks.

Sensing the change, Niamh moved away a little, her head still low. 'I'm sorry.'

'Don't be. There's nothing to be sorry about. I miss him too.'

Niamh sniffed. 'It's such a relief to hear someone talk about him like . . . like they cared. Mum tried, but she

. . . well, she doesn't like Dad much.'

'I understand.' Harriet went back to her original seat and pulled her handbag up from the floor. 'Listen, Niamh, I'm going to pay up. I think we should go back to my place and wait for your uncle there, okay? Do you want to message him and tell him? There isn't a mobile signal in the village, but the WiFi in the pub is free. If not, we can call him from my landline when we get back.'

Niamh nodded. 'Let's do that.' She still didn't look up. 'I'll just go to the loo.' She slid off her seat and headed off to the toilets, still sniffing.

5

Tim's eyes itched. Taking one hand off the wheel to rub one, he decided he really needed to stop for a break. He needed to get to Niamh as well, but crashing the car en route wouldn't help him. As he drove, he ran the conversation with that Harriet woman over in his mind. She had sounded normal. Northern, obviously, but normal. Given that she was standing next to Niamh and he had been two hundred miles away, there wasn't really much he could have done other than agree.

If only he'd paid more attention when Niamh had asked him to take her to Yorkshire! It was a cry for help, and he hadn't even recognised it. Mel was going to kill him when she found out.

With a flash of panic, he realised that he hadn't called Wendy's mother back. He'd better do that before she contacted

Mel. Shit. He had to handle this without Mel finding out or he was toast.

A motorway service station sign loomed. Right. A break, some coffee and a bit of damage limitation. Ten minutes and he'd be off again.

A few minutes later, he slumped into a plastic seat with a double espresso and called Wendy's mother to say he'd found Niamh. 'Yes. She's fine. I've got her,' he lied. 'Thank you so much for your help earlier.'

He hung up and took a sip of the scalding coffee, then tried Niamh's phone again. It went to answerphone. He felt another flutter of panic in his chest. The phone was his only live link to Niamh. Without that, he had no idea where she was. No, that wasn't strictly true. He knew she was in Trewton Royd. Correction: he *believed* she was in Trewton Royd with that Harriet woman. He didn't *know* anything.

Pulling out his phone, he put in the postcode that Harriet had given him — he must stop thinking of her as 'that

Harriet woman'. That was what Mel had called her. Harriet had taken Niamh in when she'd turned up unexpectedly. She couldn't be all that bad.

When Mel had first found out about Harriet, Tim was the first person she'd called. Hearing his sister sobbing down the phone had made him want to go and punch something — preferably Richard. Mel and Richard's marriage had been rocky for a while before that, but while Mel was trying to patch things up, Richard had taken a mistress. On the pretence of working on a project in Leeds, he had gone up there for days on end. It was the last nail in the coffin. Mel had thrown Richard out and filed for divorce soon after. Most people saw Mel as bossy and decisive. She was, but Tim also knew the other side of her. The side that needed to grab this life she had been given with both hands and make a success of it. The side that took failure as a personal affront.

After what seemed like ages, Google

Maps came up with Trewton Royd. There was hardly anything there. A long road, a few side streets. Zooming in, he found a marker for the pub.

It seemed like such a remote location. He felt another surge of anxiety. He tried Niamh's phone again. Nothing. It was hours since he'd spoken to her. Looking back at his phone, he noticed that the pub had its contact details on the web. He pressed call.

'Trewton Arms,' said a female voice.

Now that someone had answered, he wasn't sure what he had intended. He took a breath, not sure what to say.

'If this is another PPI call . . . ' said an annoyed voice at the other end.

'Hello,' he said, quickly. 'I, erm, I'm phoning to ask about a lady called Harriet Brown.'

'Oh yes, she's here. Shall I get her for you?'

'No, don't do that. I, er . . . has she got a young girl with her? Fourteen. Blonde. Green eyes.'

There was a pause. 'Who is this?'

'My name's Tim. I'm her uncle. I just wanted to check she was okay. If she's with Harriet, then that's fine.' That didn't sound great, even to him.

The woman on the other line was quiet for a minute. There was rustling as though she'd put her hand over the phone. Tim panicked and hung up. He stared at the phone for a moment, feeling like an idiot. He ran the conversation through again in his head. How to come off sounding like a weirdo.

Should he phone back and explain? Or would that make things worse? Clearly Harriet was in the pub. With Niamh. The lady from the pub was going to tell them about the call. He really should call back. Okay. If he was going to phone back, he needed to work out what he was going to say first.

He took a glug of coffee and winced at how hot it was. In his other hand, his phone rang. It was an unfamiliar number.

He put down his coffee cup. 'Hello?'

'Uncle Tim, did you just phone the Trewton Arms?' Niamh sounded just like Mel. The thought of having to explain things to Mel put icicles in Tim's veins.

'Yes,' said Tim. 'I just wanted, uh, to book a couple of rooms. For tonight. Because I'm not driving you back home in the middle of the night.' Niamh sounded more like her usual self now. That was good.

Niamh paused. 'You didn't, though, did you?'

'No. I . . . thought I should speak to Harriet first. Check everything is okay.' Thinking on his feet. This was what he should have done when he was speaking to the pub landlady.

'O-kay. Well, we're going back to Harriet's now. Just wanted to let you know. I'm fine.'

If she was able to give him this kind of attitude, then she probably *was* fine. She sounded a hell of a lot better now than she had a few hours ago. Thank goodness. It was worth embarrassing himself to find out that she was okay. 'Have you eaten?'

'Yeah. I had a burger and chips.'

'Well, hang in there. I'm coming.'

'I told you, I'm fine,' she said. 'Anyway, I'm going now. I'm on the pub phone. There's no mobile reception in this place, but you can catch me on WhatsApp when I get into range of Harriet's WiFi. Okay? Bye.' She hung up.

Tim put his phone away and picked up his coffee again. Some of the tension lifted from his shoulders. It was a relief that Niamh was no longer distraught and alone. But he still needed to get her back home before Mel found out. Tim drained his still-hot coffee and set off back to the car. The sooner he got there, the better.

★ ★ ★

Harriet unlocked the door at the top of the stairs and let Niamh into the flat. The teenager ambled in, stopped and looked around. 'It looks different.'

'Different?' Harriet turned from hanging up her coat.

'I've been here before,' she said. 'When I came up with Dad, remember?' She put her head to one side. 'Maybe it was because it was summer last time. And in the daytime.'

Harriet scanned the room and suddenly saw it from someone else's eyes. When Niamh had last been in the flat, it had been tidy. She had made an effort, tidied up, put throws over the sofa, even put a bunch of flowers in a vase, she remembered. It had looked homely.

Now it looked tired and neglected. Washing was draped over radiators. Post, magazines, dirty mugs and one of last night's wine bottles were on the floor next to the sofa. Before, it had been the small but quirky flat of a professional freelancer; now it looked like a nest. For the first time, she noticed that the place smelled of stale wine and toast.

'Daylight makes all the difference,' Harriet said. She scooped up the empty

68

bottle and mugs and pushed the magazines under the coffee table with her foot. 'Here. Take a seat.'

She dumped the mugs in the sink. She'd wash them later. 'Can I get you anything? It'll be a long wait for your uncle to get here.'

Niamh shook her head. She didn't sit down, but walked over to a photo of Richard and Harriet in Blackpool. She picked it up. 'He looks happy,' she said.

Harriet went across and stood next to her. 'He was . . . we were.'

'Do you miss him?' Niamh's voice was a broken whisper.

'Every minute of every day.'

Niamh nodded and sniffed. Poor kid. Harriet couldn't believe that Mel could be so insensitive towards her daughter. How could she not see how much Niamh missed her father? She put her arms around the girl and gently pulled her into a hug. Niamh was still for a moment, awkward, then her forehead rested on Harriet's shoulder and her whole body shook in a huge sob. It was as though a dam had broken. These were not quiet tears like the ones in the pub. These were ugly, primal tears of a broken heart. Niamh clung to Harriet and wept. Harriet held her, rocking gently. She would have to have words with Mel.

She'd never spoken to Mel before, because Mel hadn't been relevant to her and Richard. But Niamh had turned up on her doorstep, uninvited and in need of help. This changed things. If she'd had a child, she would have cared for them a hell of a lot better than this! And that uncle! What was his name? Tim? What kind of a feckless idiot allowed a teenager to travel halfway across the country without even noticing that they'd gone?

Standing in her living room with her arms around Richard's daughter, Harriet suddenly felt something shift inside her. The woman she used to be, before the crushing blackness of grief had buried her, looked out. And was horrified. The flat hadn't been cleaned in months. There was no reason for her to live like this. Working in the corner shop, for heaven's sake. Didn't she have a business of her own to run?

All this wallowing in self-pity wasn't going to bring Richard back. She had to move on. But first, this child needed her. If Richard couldn't be there for Niamh, Harriet would have to do her best to fill the breach.

6

Tim turned off the radio so that he could concentrate on the road signs. He had come off the motorway onto empty roads. It was nearly midnight, so it wasn't surprising that everything was deserted, but it still felt weird.

The satnav guided him higher into the hills, away from the towns, until he was driving along seemingly endless roads in pitch-black countryside. Every so often, the moon would appear for long enough to show him moorland or the occasional dark building in the distance. At last he crested a hill and descended into what looked like a collection of houses in a single main road. He passed a sign that read 'Trewton Royd welcomes careful drivers'. The road down was so steep he had to shift down a gear to maintain control.

The village was dark apart from a short row of street lights that showed closed shops. He spotted the corner shop and parked opposite. It was past midnight. He peered at the shop. Harriet had mentioned a door around the side. A few steps in the damp darkness and he found it.

His knock sounded over-loud in the quiet street. Maybe he should have called her instead. He looked up the road. A cat ran across the tarmac, otherwise there was no movement. Tim shivered; now that the residual warmth from the car had seeped away, it was really cold.

Footsteps, like someone coming down stairs . . . and the door opened, spilling light over him. A figure stood silhouetted against the light.

Tim opened his mouth, but before he could speak, the figure had pulled him inside.

'Uh . . . Harriet?' he said.

'Yes. And you're Tim,' she said. 'Shh. Niamh is asleep. Come on up.'

His eyes adjusted to the light as he

followed a denim-clad bottom up the stairs. Not that he was looking at her bum, but it was hard to avoid it when it was a few steps above him. He shook his head, trying to clear his jumbled thoughts.

At the top of the stairs was a tiny landing. Harriet put a finger to her lips and opened the door to the flat. Feeling as though the situation had somehow got away from him, Tim followed her. He took in the small living room. The room was warmly lit by lamps and light from a kitchen that was off to the side.

Niamh was asleep on the sofa, one arm hooked under a cushion. She was covered by a couple of fleece blankets.

He tiptoed up to her and hunkered down. She seemed unhurt. Tim let out a breath. She looked okay. And so very young. Close up, he could see her face was puffy from crying. He gently pushed her hair off her face. She didn't even stir. Poor Niamh. She'd had a hell of a day.

A movement on the other side of the

room made him look up. Harriet had gone into the kitchen and, judging by the sounds, was putting the kettle on. Tim stood up carefully. Now that he knew that Niamh was physically okay, the vice of fear in his throat loosened. Other emotions rushed in. Anger being the main one.

Who was he angry with? Niamh? Himself? This Harriet woman?

Being angry with Harriet would be easy. She had, after all, been instrumental in the breakup of his sister's marriage. She had seduced Richard away from Mel and put paid to any chance of reconciliation there might have been. He looked back towards Niamh, who sniffed in her sleep. Yet, this woman had taken in Niamh. It appeared she'd been kind to her. Whatever Harriet had done to Mel, when Niamh needed her, she had risen to the occasion. If he was going to be angry with anyone, it would have to be with himself.

He'd already screwed up enough to

let this happen. Now he needed to man up and fix things. First of all, he needed to thank Harriet. He took a deep breath and approached the kitchen.

Harriet was staring into the steam that was escaping from the kettle, apparently deep in thought. Tim got a good look at her for the first time. His memory of her was of a weak, droopy woman in black, seen at a distance. This woman was not droopy. In fact, her back was very straight. Tense. She was dressed in jeans and a sweater that was slightly too large. The sleeves had been pushed back to reveal slim forearms. Her hair was escaping from the loose bun it had been gathered into. Overall, she gave the impression of controlled chaos. Messy, maybe, but not droopy.

The kettle made a weird knocking sound and steam billowed out. Harriet blinked and seemed to notice Tim for the first time. 'Tea or coffee?' she said.

'That's very kind of you, but I should really wake Niamh up and get — '

'The poor child is exhausted.' She

dropped the kettle back onto its base with a clack. 'You're not taking her anywhere.' She turned, eyes flashing. 'Seriously? Mel left her child with you?'

Tim took a tiny step back. 'I . . . ' For a moment, he didn't know how to respond to her verbal attack. Tiredness and self-defence came to his rescue. No, this woman didn't get to tell him off. He'd driven all the way up here to get Niamh. He was bloody well taking her home. 'Look. I appreciate what you've done, but Niamh is my responsibility. I have to take her home.'

'You're right, she was your responsibility. So how come she ended up two hundred miles away before you noticed she'd gone?' Harriet crossed her arms and glared at him, challenging him to answer.

'I thought she was at a holiday club. I dropped her off there. She must have hidden behind the door and sneaked back out after I drove off. She even got some guy to call them and tell them she was ill.' His voice crept up to normal volume and he hastily modulated it. 'How was I to compete with orchestrated deception like that?'

Harriet glared at him some more. There was something in that glare that made him feel about six years old.

He tried again. 'Look,' he said, spreading his hands in a placating gesture. 'I'm really sorry about all the hassle this must have caused you. I'd been trying to call her. She finally picked up to say she was in Huddersfield and I jumped in the car and came straight here. Thank you so much for looking after her, but I need to get her home. Her mother is going to kill us both when she finds out.'

At the mention of Mel, something akin to disgust flitted across Harriet's face. 'Do you even know why she ran away?'

Tim opened his mouth to argue that he did, but realised he had no idea. Not really. He hazarded a guess. 'She was missing her father and wanted to talk to you about him.' Which was roughly what Niamh had said days ago, when they'd had the conversation-cum-argument about it. Again, he mentally kicked himself for not agreeing to take her then.

Harriet rolled her eyes. 'Yes, but why did she need to talk to me about him? She's only met me once.'

'Because you were Richard's mistress — '

'Girlfriend,' she corrected him.

He inclined his head. Fine. Whatever she wanted to label herself.

'It's not because I was his girlfriend,' Harriet carried on. 'It's because she didn't feel she could talk to anyone else. The girl has lost her father. She's scared she's forgetting him and her own mother refuses to talk to her about him. What kind of a heartless bitch does that?'

'She's not a heartless bitch.' The only person who got to be rude to Mel was him. 'She's got a lot of things going on at the mo — '

'Things more important than a child struggling to cope with a bereavement?

Niamh is fourteen, for heaven's sake. How is she supposed to cope with this sort of thing on her own?'

'She's had counselling . . . ' Even to his own ears that sounded feeble. Mel had told him about this. She had seemed to think that was exactly what Niamh needed. In fact, he'd thought Niamh was looking happier for it. Tim loved his niece, but he assumed that Mel knew what was best for her. What if she didn't? Should he have paid more attention? Been more involved? He thought of Mel. She wouldn't take kindly to his interfering.

Harriet gave a snort. 'Counselling.' She thrust a mug at him. 'You're lucky she ran away to me and didn't just disappear.'

Which was true. 'Yes, well. Like I said, thank you. I'm very grateful — '

She brushed past him and left the kitchen. He stared after her. Did she ever allow anyone to finish a sentence? It was like having a conversation with an Uzi.

Harriet twitched a curtain aside and

peered out of the window. 'The lights are still on in the pub,' she said. 'You'll be able to find a room there.' She nodded across to Niamh, who was still asleep. 'Let her sleep here tonight. She's knackered, poor thing. I'll give her some breakfast and call you to come get her in the morning.'

He should argue. He should insist that he couldn't leave his niece with her, a stranger.

'She came to me.' It was as though Harriet had read his mind. 'Right now, Niamh trusts me more than she trusts you.' She levelled her peculiarly intense gaze at him. 'If you let her stay here, at least we can both be sure where she is come the morning.'

She looked across at him, face tilted, daring him to challenge her. Mel would be furious with him if he left Niamh with Harriet. He wanted to rise to the challenge. To flare up and soar to her level. But he was exhausted. Now that he knew Niamh was safe, the adrenaline that had driven him drained out and left him hollow. Tim rubbed a hand over his eyes. He offered up a silent apology to his sister and sighed. Harriet had a point. Niamh was safe here. She'd been here most of the night, so a few hours more wouldn't make much difference.

'Okay, fine,' he said. 'I'll come over as soon as I can in the morning.' He glanced across at his niece. 'Please, don't let her out of your sight.'

Harriet stepped away from the window and stood beside him, also looking down at Niamh. 'I'll look after her,' she said quietly. 'Don't worry. She's Richard's daughter. She'll be safe with me.'

Tim glanced sideways at her. He believed her. Whatever Mel said about this woman, Richard had cared about her and he had introduced Niamh to her. Niamh felt safe enough with her to run across the country to come and see her. He nodded. 'Okay. Thank you.'

7

Harriet woke up and winced out of habit before realising her head didn't hurt. She hauled herself upright. She felt tired, but . . . different. The events of the night before came back in a rush. Niamh. She sprang out of bed and ran into the living room, suddenly dreading that she'd dreamt it all. That Niamh was just a proxy that her messed-up mind had substituted for Richard, because dreaming about Richard every night wasn't bad enough.

But Niamh was still curled up on the sofa. Still real. Still asleep. An immense sense of relief washed over Harriet. She slumped against the wall. Everything from last night had really happened. Niamh had reached out to her for help and she'd responded like a fully functioning adult. To do anything else would have let Richard down.

She dressed and crept downstairs to run the papers across to the pub. The shop didn't open for a while yet, but the punters at the pub liked their papers nice and early. The pub reception was empty, so she popped them behind the desk and got back. She finished off her early tasks and went back upstairs to go have a shower and wake up properly.

By the time she was ready, light glared through the small gap in the curtains. Harriet checked the time. Eight o'clock. Niamh was still asleep. She shook her head and crept back to her room.

She should call Tim at the pub and let him know that Niamh was okay. She would have to phone the pub reception to get the number for his room. He had also taken her number. Harriet sank onto her bed and put her face in her hands.

Niamh wanted to talk about her dad. She was working through her grief, desperate to make sure she remembered him. Harriet recognised the feeling. That fleeting moment when she couldn't quite remember the shape of his face or the exact timbre of his voice. The horror that one day she wouldn't be able to recall him at all. She had tried to reassure Niamh that this was normal. That for every moment of fading, there would be one of absolute clarity, when it felt like he was still alive, just about to walk into the room. This happened to Harriet, but would it really happen for Niamh?

Where Harriet lived in a place that was steeped in Richard, Niamh lived with a woman who hated talking about him. From what she'd said, there were no photos dotted around the place, no little mementoes. While Harriet could, and frequently did, pretend that Richard was not dead, that he would show up on Friday and stay for the weekend, Niamh couldn't do that. Poor kid.

Counselling. Pah. That Mel was the one who needed her head seeing to.

Then there was this Tim guy. Harriet glanced at her cordless phone. She really should get in touch and tell him that Niamh was still here, but sleeping in like the teenager she was.

She wasn't sure what to make of Tim. He was Mel's twin brother, so she'd been expecting someone brisk and abrasive, but all she'd seen last night was a man who was frantic with worry for his niece. His face when he knelt in front of her to check if she was okay . . . he seemed kind. Not at all like the unthinking evil sidekick that she had expected.

What had Richard said about him? Nothing much, she decided. Tim. Mel's brother. Academic. Quiet. Irrelevant. And now he was here. Which made him a bit more relevant.

The phone rang. She snatched it up, knowing it was going to be Tim.

'She's still here. She's fine,' she said instead of a greeting.

'Oh good,' said Tim, relief evident in his voice. 'Is she awake?'

'She's fourteen. What do you think?'

'Oh, right. I was going to have

breakfast and then — '

'I need to go to work by nine.' Well, half nine would do, but it was best to keep a little leeway.

'I'll be there before nine.'

She should just hand Niamh over to his care and leave them to it . . . but Niamh needed to talk about her father, to keep her happy memories of him. Harriet thought of the girl's green eyes, so like her father's. Truth be told, Harriet needed to talk about Richard too. Seeing Niamh again . . . it was as though a little part of Richard had been returned to her. She needed Niamh to stay, at least for a little bit longer. Tim was not going to like that.

Harriet shrugged and got to her feet. Tough.

★ ★ ★

Tim was still groggy when he went downstairs for breakfast. The pub was quiet. There were a few couples finishing off their food and poring over maps. The table that had the best view from the window was occupied by a girl with a blue stripe in her hair. Tim chose a table at the edge of the room.

The landlady bustled in. 'Hello, love. I'm Angie. I didn't meet you last night. It was very late when you got in.'

'Yes. I'm so sorry to have bothered your husband at that time of night.'

'Oh, don't you worry about it,' she said. 'Harriet warned us that you'd be late getting here. Have you come far?'

'From Reading.'

'That's quite a drive,' she said. 'Especially if you're not staying long. You should make a weekend of it. See the sights.'

'Um. I have to get back . . . ' He stopped talking. If he said much more, he'd have to explain why he was there and then his shockingly bad *in loco parentis* skills would come to light.

The landlady seemed to sense his reluctance. 'Anyway, what can I get you for breakfast, love?'

He ordered an egg muffin and a pot

of coffee. He wished he'd bought a newspaper. Or bothered to log on to the pub's WiFi. There was no mobile signal and he didn't have much in data on his contract — why bother when he had free WiFi where he worked? He would have to ask the landlady for the WiFi password. With nothing to do, he ended up watching the other people in the room instead.

A man who looked Indian walked past him and took a seat opposite the girl with the blue stripe in her hair. Tim couldn't see her face, but her stance relaxed immediately. He said something and the girl laughed.

Tim felt a sudden pang of envy. What must it be like to have someone who understood and complemented you. Someone so comfortable to be with. He had had that once, but now it was gone. With a start, he realised that the person he was thinking of wasn't Sarah, but his best friend. He missed Nick more than he missed Sarah.

The landlady reappeared with his

order and put it in front of him. He thanked her and turned to his food, expecting her to leave.

'So, how do you know Harriet, then?' she asked.

'I don't, really. Not very well. My niece knows her though. They're . . . friends.'

'Oh, that girl that was in here with Harriet last night. She cried a lot last night, I think. I saw Harriet giving her a hug. Is she all right?'

Niamh had been crying. If anything, he felt worse now. Poor Niamh. It was probably a good thing that she had been asleep when he got there, otherwise he might have been stupid enough to have a go at her for running off. Clearly, there was stuff going on with Niamh that he didn't understand. Her mother didn't understand either, by the sounds of things. 'She's okay. She stayed over at Harriet's last night.'

Angie gave a sniff. The sort of sniff that suggested that she wouldn't have let Niamh stay at Harriet's.

Tim couldn't ignore that. He put his fork down. 'You don't like Harriet?' he asked, old anxieties resurfacing.

Angie gave a shrug. 'She's okay,' she said carefully. 'You'll like her. Men usually do.'

Tim frowned. 'But you don't approve of Niamh staying with her. Why is that?'

Angie looked around and lowered her voice. 'Between you and me and the gatepost, Harriet's been acting a bit strange lately.'

Uh oh. He leaned forward. 'Strange? How do you mean?' He tried to keep the rising panic out of his voice. Had he left his niece with some unbalanced weirdo?

'Well . . . ' Angie pulled a face. 'Not her usual self, if you see what I mean. She used to do some working online thing, so she'd be out and about during the day. You know, pop into the coffee shop and the like. Then, about a year ago, she stopped doing all that. Went a bit quiet. Started working at the shop. And going out drinking.' Angie shook her head. 'I reckon she broke up with her fella and took it a bit too hard.'

He tried to follow all this and reconcile it with the fierce woman he'd met the night before. 'I'm sure there's a reasonable explanation,' he said carefully. He sifted through the information Angie had just spilled out. So Richard and Harriet had split up sometime before Richard died. That must have been some acrimonious breakup. Funny that Richard hadn't mentioned it. Mel had assumed that Richard was on his way to Yorkshire to see Harriet when the accident happened, but maybe he hadn't been. He wondered what Mel would make of that.

'Funny though,' said Angie thoughtfully. 'I thought they looked really happy the last time I saw them together. That were a while ago, mind.' She smiled. 'Anyway. How does your niece know her, then?'

'Her father used to be Harriet's partner. A couple of years ago.' It sounded like there had been a few men in Harriet's life, so he added, 'Richard.'

'She's Richard's little girl? Oh my, I didn't recognise her. Hasn't she grown? She was only about twelve when she came to stay that time.'

Richard had brought Niamh to this place? This was news to Tim. He wondered if Mel knew. He looked at his rapidly cooling breakfast and picked up a forkful.

Angie carried on, 'So why is she here? Is she trying to get Richard and Harriet back together, you think?'

Tim paused in the act of putting the egg in his mouth. He lowered it. Harriet hadn't even seen fit to tell people that Richard had died? 'Um, Richard . . . he, er . . . Richard died. About a year ago.'

Angle's hand flew to her mouth. 'No. She never said! When he stopped coming to visit, we all assumed . . . ' Her hand fluttered down to lie over her heart. 'Poor Harriet. But why didn't she say anything?'

Which was a good question. If Harriet hadn't broken up with Richard

. . . Tim mentally rewound the conversation. Harriet had started acting weird after Richard died, but hadn't told anyone about his death, so everyone had assumed he had split up with her and put her behaviour down to some sort of post-breakup trauma. But why would she keep something like that a secret?

Tim watched as, before his eyes, Angie recast Harriet from object of scorn to object of pity. He felt like he was watching something momentous.

Angie turned and addressed the couple in the window. 'Did you know that Harriet's boyfriend died last year?' she demanded.

They looked surprised. 'Why on earth would we know anything about it?' said the girl with the blue striped hair.

'You're young. And you get on well with her, Vinnie, don't you?' Angie insisted.

'She's never mentioned . . . ' said the guy. 'That's really sad. Maybe she

94

doesn't like to talk about it. Grief takes people that way sometimes.'

Tim suddenly felt bad. Small villages were rife with gossip. Harriet had clearly not wanted everyone to know and now everyone would know. Within minutes, if this morning was anything to go by. He reminded himself that Harriet had broken up his sister's marriage. He shouldn't feel bad. He really shouldn't.

'Perhaps,' said the guy called Vinnie, 'she didn't want everyone to be gossiping about it behind her back.'

'I can understand that,' said the girl. 'Maybe it's best not to mention it, Auntie Angie.'

'But . . . ' The landlady looked stricken.

'Maybe don't tell anyone else in the village yet,' the girl added. 'I'm sure Harriet had her reasons for keeping it quiet.'

Angie frowned. 'I suppose,' she said. Then, after a moment's reflection, she added, 'She's always been there for us when we've needed anything. We'll be there for her.' That decided, she gave Tim a friendly nod. 'I hope your niece is feeling better.' She smiled at him and wandered off, still looking thoughtful.

Tim glanced across at the couple in the window. The guy raised his eyebrows. 'Don't worry about it,' he said. 'Village politics. You get used to it.'

★ ★ ★

Harriet banged around in the kitchen, which had the desired effect of waking Niamh up.

'Morning,' Harriet said cheerfully. 'I've made coffee.' She plonked a mug of it in front of Niamh. 'How're you feeling this morning?'

Niamh sat up and rubbed her eyes. 'My head hurts a little.' She pulled the coffee towards her. 'Apart from that, I'm good.'

'Your uncle showed up last night,' said Harriet, watching the girl carefully to see her reaction.

96

Niamh looked worried, but not scared. 'Am I in terrible trouble? Has he told Mum?'

'Yes and no. I mean yes, you're probably in trouble, but no, I don't think he's told your mum.' Harriet sat down in the chair opposite Niamh. 'Listen, I have to go and open the shop in a few minutes. I want you to make yourself at home. Use the shower. Whatever you need. I'm just down-stairs.' She took a deep breath and then let it out. 'I know your uncle is going to want to take you home now, but I want you to know that you're welcome here for as long as you like. Okay?'

Niamh stared at her coffee for a moment. 'Thank you,' she said quietly. Bright green eyes looked up at Harriet. 'I don't want to go home. Not yet. I feel . . . I want to explore here. Dad loved it in this village. He went on about how lovely and relaxing it was and showed me pictures of the church and the pub and things. I mean, I know he came here because he wanted to be with you, but I think he also really liked the place. I want to see it, you know, see if I feel what he felt. It might make me feel a little closer to him.' She flushed. 'Does that even make sense?'

Harriet, who still kept Richard's pyjamas in her chest of drawers and his toothbrush in the bathroom, nodded. 'It makes sense to me.'

She wanted to add that Niamh herself made Harriet feel closer to Richard, like he'd sent her so that they could heal each other, but she stopped herself. Saying it out loud was a step too far. She glanced up at the clock on the wall behind Niamh. 'Oh heck, I'd better get going. If you need anything, just nip downstairs. There's a connecting door to the shop.' She grabbed the keys to the shop, picked up her coffee in the other hand, and headed for the door. 'Really, if you need anything at all, just come and get me.'

★　★　★

Tim tried messaging Niamh again before he stepped out of the pub. No answer. She had seen his first WhatsApp message though, according to the two ticks against it. She was probably sulking. Sighing, he slipped the phone into his pocket and stepped outside.

When he'd arrived, it had been too dark to see anything. Now, in the weak sunshine, the village gleamed at him. It was like he'd stepped into a postcard. The hills rose up on either side, hemming the sky with green. He looked up and remembered the heart-stopping incline he'd driven down. It hadn't been his imagination. It really was that steep. The main road threaded its way through the village and up over the next hill. The pub faced a fork in the road that led off towards a picture-perfect church with the valley behind it. A cherry tree was in full bloom just outside the pub. It couldn't have looked more beautiful. Tim took a deep breath, letting the sharp air fill his lungs. Richard had called this place idyllic.

For the first time, Tim understood what he'd meant.

It only took a minute to walk across to Harriet's place. Tim knocked on the side door before he realised that the shop was open and tried there instead. A bell above the door tinkled when he entered. It was a small corner shop, no more than a few aisles. Harriet was talking to a customer, a young woman with a pushchair. He watched her as she talked, observing her in full daylight for the first time.

His only real measure of Harriet was from what Mel had told him. She spoke of some parochial northern harpy who had ensnared Richard with her big boobs and empty head. From what he'd seen of her last night, Harriet, whilst certainly northern, was sharp-tongued and assertive, not quite the airhead Mel had made her out to be. She was tall and her hair was a reddish brown. Looking at her now, he thought she was probably in her late thirties, or early forties at most. A treacherous part of him noted that Harriet was quite attractive. He tried to ignore that. He had to focus on getting Niamh back to Reading before Mel figured out something was wrong.

The customer left and Harriet looked in his direction. She nodded towards a door in the side wall of the shop. 'She's in the flat,' she said. 'Just head up the stairs and knock.'

He approached the counter. 'I just wanted to say thank you. If you hadn't picked Niamh up from the station last night, who knows what might have happened.'

She avoided his eyes and brushed his thanks away. 'Anyone would have done the same.'

He wanted to ask her why she hadn't told anyone about Richard's death. Why was it better to have been dumped by him than to have lost him in a car accident? But he didn't know her well enough.

Instead, he said, 'And thanks for feeding her. Look, do I owe you anything? For — '

'No, you're all right.' She began shuffling postcards and local maps near the till, tidying them even though they didn't need tidying.

'Right. Well . . . thanks again.' He took a step away before turning and heading towards the side door that led to her flat.

'Tim,' Harriet called after him.

He turned back.

'If she wants to stay an extra day or two . . . she's more than welcome. It's nice to have her around.' There was something in the way she said it that made it sound like a plea. As though she wanted Niamh to stay, but didn't want to ask. Puzzled, Tim opened the side door and headed up the steps.

He had to knock and call out to Niamh several times before she opened the door. 'Oh. Hi, Uncle Tim,' she said.

She was eating a slice of toast. Her hair was damp, suggesting she'd had a shower. He shut the door and had a good look at her, checking she was okay. She looked better than she had the night before. There were shadows under her eyes, which wasn't surprising considering how late she'd been up. Her nose was a bit red, but apart from that, she looked fine. His relief told him how worried he'd been.

'Can I get you a cup of tea or anything?' said Niamh, acting for all the world as though she lived there.

Now that he knew she was okay, Tim relaxed a bit. He knew he should be angry. He would be, eventually, but not yet. First he needed to get her home. 'Seriously? Tea?' he said. 'We need to get home before your mum finds out you were even gone.'

Niamh lowered the half-eaten toast. She looked up at him from under her fringe. 'Don't be cross.'

He sighed. 'I'm not cross. I'm tired and I've had a terrible shock. Don't ever do that to me again.'

'I'm sorry.' Her eyes filled with tears.

He held out his arms to her and she buried her face in his chest. When had she become so tall?

'You understand, though, right?' she said into his shoulder. 'Why I had to come.'

He patted her back. In a way, he did understand. It was hard to let someone go. He knew what it was like to say goodbye to someone he loved. He had said goodbye to Mel once. Things had worked out and he'd never actually lost her, though. So what did he know, truly? 'I'm not sure I do, Niamh. I'm just glad you're okay.'

'I don't want to go home just yet,' said Niamh.

'We have to.'

'But look at this place.' Niamh took a step back from him and waved an arm. 'Dad was here. There are pictures of him and notes with his handwriting on and stuff that he used. He used to sit in that chair. That's his favourite mug. Harriet remembers him. She's not trying to deny he ever existed, like Mum tries to. I need to be here. Just a bit longer. Please. I need to.'

He looked around and tried to see the flat as she saw it, as a memorial to her father. All he saw was a slightly neglected place which looked like any other one-bedroom flat.

'You can't impose on Harriet,' he said. 'She didn't invite you here. It's one thing to stay over in an emergency. To stay longer would just be taking advantage.'

'Harriet said I could stay as long as I wanted. I think she liked talking about Dad too.'

If she wants to stay an extra day or two . . . she's more than welcome. It sounded like Harriet felt that way too. Maybe if this had all been cleared with Mel beforehand, he and Niamh could have made a weekend of it. Heaven knew he couldn't remember the last time he'd taken some time off. But the way things were, the sooner he got her home, the better.

'I'm sorry, Niamh, but we really need to get you home before your mum finds out about all this. It's bad enough if she hears that you ran away, but if she realises you were here . . . '

Niamh's face lost what little colour it had. 'You're not going to tell her, are you?'

'Of course not. But she's going to find out. We're in a place with no mobile phone coverage. The longer we stay here, the more likely it is that she'll find out.'

Niamh eyed him thoughtfully and he realised he'd made a mistake. He should have kept the threat of telling Mel as an inducement. Dammit. Now that she knew he wasn't intending to tell Mel, he was as good as sucked in to her escapade.

'Who else knows I'm not at home?' she said. 'Wendy won't tell.'

'I spoke to Wendy's mum last night and told her I'd found you.'

'You spoke to Wendy's mum?' A flare of panic. 'Why?'

'Why d'you think? You disappeared. I thought you'd been abducted or something. Honestly, Niamh. Did you really think you could just run off like that without me trying to find you? I nearly had the police out looking for you.'

'Seriously?'

'Seriously.' Good God, the child had no concept of what she had put him through. Perhaps she was more like Mel than she realised.

Niamh looked up at him, her eyes huge. 'I'm sorry, Uncle Tim. I'm really sorry I scared you. It was a stupid thing to have done, but you have to understand — it was worth it. I needed to talk to someone about Dad . . . I needed to be in the places he'd been. It's important.' Her eyes glittered with the hint of tears. 'I'm scared . . . I think I might be forgetting him.' She put a hand on his arm. 'That's why I need to stay here a bit longer. Just a day or two. I want to walk in the places he walked. See the things he saw. He really loved this place. Not just Harriet, but the place. It was special.'

'No. No, Niamh. We're going home.'

'One day, then, Uncle Tim. Just one

more day. I promise I'll be really well behaved. I won't go anywhere without telling you. Just one more day.' She gazed up at him with big pleading eyes full of tears. 'Please, Uncle Tim. Please.'

He looked down at her and it was like seeing Mel when she was a child. *Please, Tim, please. If you don't do this for me, I might die.* He had never had the heart to refuse. She had stopped doing that now that she was an adult, but the tone of voice still had the same effect on him. He always ended up doing what she wanted. Always. It seemed that Niamh had the same skill. Damn.

Besides, Niamh made a good point. He could understand that she needed time to feel close to her dad. He could well believe that Mel didn't like to talk about Richard. Mel had been deeply hurt by her divorce from Richard and the only reason she had anything to do with him was because he needed access to Niamh. Niamh was clearly unhappy. Maybe, by giving her a few days here, she might be able to find some closure

. . . or at least comfort.

He frowned. He would have to square this with Mel later. For all her bossiness, his sister always came round to doing the right thing. At this moment in time, the right thing for Niamh was to be here.

'Fine,' he said. 'We'll stay the weekend. We go home on Sunday, no arguments. Okay?'

'Yes.'

'And you're not staying here. I'm booking a room for you in the pub. That is not negotiable.'

She threw her arms around him again and gave him a hard squeeze. 'Thank you, thank you, thank you, Uncle Tim. You're the best.'

He smiled at the top of her head. 'Yeah, well. First of all though, we need to work out how we're going to keep this from your mum until we're ready. If she finds out now, she'll abandon her retreat and come haring over here.'

'I have an idea,' said Niamh. She grabbed her jacket. 'Come on.'

8

After a brief flurry of activity, the shop was quiet again. Harriet picked up the reduced stickers. May as well hunt down the things that were going to expire soon. This was one of the jobs she really liked. Once things had passed their sell by date, she had to keep them around for a few days, and then she could throw them away or take them for herself. If something had a longish shelf life to start with, they were still fine a few days past their best-by date.

The side door opened and Niamh bounced in, followed by a slightly bemused-looking Tim.

'Uncle Tim said I could stay for the weekend,' said Niamh.

Oh good. Harriet searched Niamh's face for signs of Richard and found only a few, but the sight of those green eyes were enough. The sense of connection to Richard made her feel better, more alive than she had felt in months.

'I've booked us rooms in the pub, so we won't be in your way,' said Tim. He was looking at Niamh when he said this, as though referring to some earlier conversation.

'We're going to go explore the village now,' said Niamh. 'Would you mind if we met up with you later in the afternoon, Harriet? Only if it's no bother.'

'I . . . um. I finish here at twelve,' she said. 'I can meet you any time afterward.'

'Shall we arrange a time and a place? We don't want you to be hanging around waiting for us,' said Tim.

Tim, she noticed, had blue eyes. She wondered if Niamh's mother's eyes were blue. When she'd met Mel at the funeral, the colour of her eyes had been the last thing on her mind.

'Just pop by any time,' said Harriet. 'I'll be at home.' Then, realising how sad that sounded, she added, 'I'll be doing some work, but it's nothing that can't be interrupted.' In reality, she would probably be watching daytime TV or browsing the internet. Ugh. What had her life become? When was the last time she'd actually done any copywriting work?

'Okay. We'll come round at about four then,' said Tim.

'Where's the best place to get a mobile signal around here?' said Niamh, taking out her phone. 'Some of my friends' parents force them to have these really lame phones with no data. They still use texts.' She rolled her eyes like she couldn't believe people still relied on the phone network when there was WiFi available.

'Top of the hill.' Harriet pointed. 'You'd have come into the village that way.'

'I know it,' said Tim. 'It's very steep.'

'I'm sure you'll manage to struggle up it.' Niamh grinned at her uncle.

'I'll manage just fine,' said Tim. He shooed her out of the shop. 'I bet I'm fitter than you are.'

They left, still bickering and teasing each other. Harriet watched them leave and felt thankful that she would get to see Richard's daughter again. She leaned against the counter and sighed. Had Richard, looking out for her from wherever he was, sent Niamh to her? Harriet dropped her head. She was being fanciful.

Ash appeared from somewhere at the back of the shop and watched Niamh's departing back. 'Who,' he said, 'was that?'

Harriet turned to stare at him, surprised at the sudden burst of protectiveness she felt towards Niamh. 'She's too young for you,' she said, raising her eyebrows at him.

He held his hands up. 'I was only asking.'

*   *   *

They walked out of the shop and turned to climb the hill, Tim in front. A few hundred yards up the incline and Niamh was already starting to puff. 'This is steep.'

'Oh come on, I thought you young people were supposed to be fit,' said Tim.

She gave him a look that should have fried him.

A few minutes later, Tim's thigh muscles were burning. He pulled off his thin jacket and looped it over his arm. Niamh stopped and leaned against the dry stone wall and bent over, hands on her knees. 'How much further?'

Tim pulled out his phone and waved it around. 'Not far.'

They puffed on, past a row of small cottages. Niamh gestured towards them as though she were going to say something, then seemed to think better of it. A few more yards and a single bar of signal appeared on Tim's phone. It buzzed as it picked up messages.

Niamh's phone was buzzing and beeping madly. She stopped and pulled it out of her pocket.

Tim pointed to a lane leading off the main road. There was a stile a short way along. They headed across to it. Niamh's head was already bent over her phone. Tim leaned against the stile and got his breath back. Below them, the village nestled in the picture postcard valley. If it was this pretty when the sky was grey, it must be stunning in full sunlight.

Now that they were near the top of the hill, the wind was stronger. If he hadn't been so hot from the climb, Tim would have needed his jacket and maybe a scarf.

'Okay,' he said when his heart rate had slowed back down to normal, 'what's this plan?'

Niamh looked up from her screen. 'We'll tell Mum that we feel very strongly that she needs to take the 'no phones' rule in this retreat seriously, so you and I are both going to refuse to answer any calls from her. For her own good.'

He was impressed. That actually

sounded like it could work. Who knew that Niamh could be so devious! 'Okay,' he said, nodding. 'Who's going to tell her that, me or you?'

She gave him a look he couldn't decipher. 'I'll do it.' She checked her phone. 'I've got a few text messages from her. From really early this morning. Not really a problem. I can just say I was asleep until late and didn't bother replying. How about you? Any messages from Mum that we need to account for?'

'I spoke to her last night.' He double checked anyway. 'Yeah, we're clear.'

'Great. Let me do this.' She made the call and stared into the middle distance with her phone to her ear, waiting for her mother's answerphone to kick in.

Tim looked through a few of the work emails that were waiting for him. His shoulders scrunched up just from seeing the contents of his inbox. He turned his phone off. He had turned his out of office message on this morning. There was nothing that couldn't wait, he was sure.

Beside him, Niamh left a message for Mel. 'Hi, Mum. I've been talking to Uncle Tim and we both reckon you're not getting the full benefit of your very expensive relaxation retreat if you're calling us at all hours. So we've got a plan to help. We're going to ignore all your calls. We'll pick up your messages at lunchtime every day, but not at any other time. So if you want to talk to us, you'll have to try at lunchtime. Otherwise, you just hang out with Alex and chill, okay? Mmm. That's it, really. Have a great time. I love you. Bye!' She hung up and raised her eyebrows at Tim. 'That should do it.'

'Where did you learn to lie so well?' he said.

She shrugged.

'Who did you get to call the holiday club?' Had it only been yesterday? It felt like weeks ago.

Niamh had the decency to look abashed. 'I paid the guy in the newsagent's a fiver to call the holiday club and Wendy's mum.'

He stared at her, not sure what to say. No wonder he hadn't had a clue when she ran away. He was not equipped to deal with this level of deception.

Niamh's lips pressed together as though she were bracing herself for another telling off. He had already given her a lecture on the danger she had put herself in. There wasn't much point doing it again. Tim sighed. 'Don't ever do anything like that again,' he said.

He looked away. The clouds over the valley were darkening. It felt almost like twilight, despite it being mid-morning.

When he looked back, Niamh was back at her phone, texting. He looked over the valley again. Was it his imagination, or did it suddenly seem even darker than before? He frowned and turned to look back over his shoulder. Oh crap. A huge black cloud had come over the hills in the time that they had been there. There was a faint hiss and the wind smelled of wet earth. Rain.

'Niamh, it's going to rain.' He nudged her and pointed. 'Let's get back.'

She turned. Her eyes went round.

They hurried back to the road and were just passing the cottages when the rain caught them. There was no preamble. It went from dry to sodden in thirty seconds. Tim pulled his jacket on as quickly as he could, but by the time he grappled with the zip, his front was already wet. Niamh, who had tied her coat around her waist, fared even worse. She pulled her hood up and they both started to run down the hill.

Running downhill wasn't easy. Niamh tripped and slammed into Tim, throwing him against the stone wall by the side of the road. His elbow banged into the stone, making him cry out.

'I'm sorry. Sorry. Are you okay?' said Niamh, getting back to her feet.

He rubbed his elbow and winced. 'Come on.'

They started off again, slower this time. By the time they got to the village, Tim's shoes were squelching with each step. His jeans were dark with water. He had pushed his hood back so that he could see, and rain ran down past his collar. He headed towards the pub. Niamh grabbed his arm. Ow.

She pointed to the shop. 'I left my stuff there.'

What? He realised she didn't have a bag with her. Damn. They couldn't turn up at Harriet's looking like this. He started to object, but Niamh was already heading across. She was altogether too much like her mother. Tim followed her. Water ran down his face. His elbow throbbed. Great.

*   *   *

By the time Harriet finished work and went up to the flat for lunch, it was getting quite late. She trudged up the narrow stairs and let herself in. The flat felt different. Cold. The downpour outside had darkened the room, so she had to turn on the lights, despite it being technically still daytime. The electric light helped, but it didn't make the place feel any better. When she left this morning, Niamh had been there, her presence seeping into the corners of the room, filling it with vitality. Now the room felt lifeless. The only thing in it was Harriet herself and, she realised, she hadn't been fully alive in months.

Looking around, she saw not her home, but a mausoleum to a relationship that no longer existed. Photos of herself and Richard. The 'guardian angel' white feather that he'd found mysteriously sitting in his car the day they'd met. The blanket he'd bought her on a whim, now folded up on the sofa from when his daughter had used it. The toothbrush in the bathroom, the dressing gown behind the door. She had left these things as they were because she was secretly hoping it wasn't true; that Richard would just show up one day and tell her it was all a mistake. Now she knew he wasn't going to. She had always known, obviously, but it had been easier to pretend. But now, after the flat had been alive with the presence of Niamh, the emptiness was difficult to deny.

Grief punched into her chest so hard that she could barely breathe. Suffocating waves of it washed over her, until she dissolved into a sobbing mess on the floor. She cried for Richard, for the awful void he had left behind. This was not decorous weeping. This was big, ugly, animal-crying with pain and tears and snot. She hadn't cried for Richard in months and it felt as raw as it had ever done. And underneath it all, there were older sorrows. Things she'd buried, uncovered by the death of Richard.

The first time, she'd tried to erase everything that would remind her of what she'd lost, so that she wouldn't think about it. Then she'd tried to keep hold of Richard by pretending that he wasn't dead. Neither system worked. The pain remained relentless.

She had no idea how long she cried. She would have cried herself to sleep if someone hadn't banged on the door. She lifted her head and looked at the door. Who could that be? Maybe if she didn't answer, they would go away.

'Harriet?' said Niamh's voice.

Harriet pushed herself off the floor and sat up. She couldn't let Niamh see her like this. She ran a hand over her cheek and wiped the slick of tears off it. A sob made her hiccup.

There was a sotto voce conversation outside. 'Harriet, we know you're there. We're soaked through. Please, let us in,' said Niamh.

'Just a minute.' Her voice cracked. She stood up, sniffing and swallowing down residual sobs. Going over to the kitchen, she splashed water on her face and patted it dry with a paper towel. She must look awful. Suddenly very weary, she tramped over to open the door.

Niamh and Tim stood there looking as though they'd been dunked. Their coats were dark with rain and both had hair plastered to their faces. They looked concerned as they stepped into the flat.

'Are you okay?' said Niamh.

Harriet opened her mouth to say she

was fine, but another sob came out instead. Fresh tears made her vision swim. She blinked to clear them, but there were more. And more.

Niamh and Tim looked at each other and something passed between them. Firm hands took her shoulders and steered her to the sofa. Niamh sat down next to her. After a second, she got up, removed the wet coat, and sat down again, this time putting her arm around Harriet. From the kitchen came the sounds of someone putting the kettle on.

'What's wrong?' said Niamh. 'Is it . . . about Dad?'

Harriet nodded, no longer able to speak.

★ ★ ★

Tim made tea in Harriet's kitchen. It involved opening cupboards to find mugs. Harriet's cupboards didn't have a lot in them. What she had was jumbled together. He found sugar in a container marked 'tea' and a packet of teabags in the bread bin. He wasn't sure what he'd expected, but he'd assumed Richard's mistress would at least have a matching pair of mugs. He poured the boiling water over teabags and wondered when he had become such a snob.

He didn't know Harriet at all. He knew of her, mainly from Mel, but he didn't know her. Yet he'd judged her before he even met her.

A quick look through the drawers and he located the cutlery. He picked out a teaspoon. There was heart-shaped piece of card tossed among the spoons. He read it before he had time to think about it.

'Thank you for a wonderful first year together. Love R'.

He stared at the familiar handwriting that slanted backwards, just like Niamh's did, and felt something shift inside him. Richard had cared for this woman. In the same way that he had once cared for Mel.

Tim had never really bonded with

Richard. When Mel had first introduced Richard to her family, she had been completely smitten by him. Tim had been less sure, but he had to admit that overall, he'd seemed like a nice guy. Besides, Richard had been good enough for Mel, so who was he to argue? Richard had, at the time, seemed to love Mel too. Somewhere along the way, that had changed. Meeting Harriet had been the last push that he'd needed.

Tim closed the drawer quietly, wishing he hadn't had that insight into Harriet's world. He didn't want to get closer to Harriet. She was his sister's enemy. But it was hard to reconcile the weeping woman in the room next door with the ruthless one Mel had described.

He didn't know how Harriet took her tea, so he would have to take the milk out there with him. He put milk and sugar in Niamh's tea. At the doorway, he paused.

Niamh had put her arms around Harriet. Her cheek rested on Harriet's head. Tears streaked down her face, but she wasn't sobbing. She was calmly, soothingly, telling Harriet that she missed her dad too.

Niamh looked like Mel. But her manner right now was pure Richard. The gentle voice, the sympathy, the aura of all-encompassing calm. Tim realised with a start that he'd always thought of Niamh as a product of Mel. A mini-Mel in the making. He had extended all his protective instincts to include his niece and assumed that she was strong-willed, stubborn and resilient, just like her mother had been. But Mel would never have sat there and shared someone's grief, or looked at someone with that level of compassion. Mel saw the world on her terms. Although she meant well, empathy, to Mel, meant taking a guess on how she would feel if she were in that position and assuming that others felt the same. Not so, Niamh. She was her father's daughter just as much as she was her mother's. Somehow, in all the drama, he and Mel had both forgotten that.

Niamh looked up and caught his eye. She smiled and gave him a tiny nod.

He cleared his throat. 'How do you take your tea, Harriet?' he asked in as casual a voice as he could manage.

Harriet sniffed. 'Milk, please. No sugar.' Her voice was hoarse.

Niamh passed Harriet a tissue and Harriet blew her nose. 'I'm sorry,' she said. 'I didn't mean to break down like that. I just . . . miss him. So much.'

'It's okay,' said Niamh. 'I cried all over you last night. It's your turn today.'

Harriet gave a little snort of what might have been laughter.

Having added a splash of milk, Tim handed the hot mug to Harriet, who looked up at him and smiled. Her gaze took him in from head to toe. Her smile slid off. 'Oh my goodness, look at you, you're soaking.' She twisted in her seat and looked at Niamh. She put her tea down on the side table, dislodging a remote control. 'You'll catch your death walking around like that.' She rose to her feet. 'Wait here.'

Harriet disappeared into the bedroom. Tim glanced across at Niamh. 'You okay?' he said, keeping his voice low.

Niamh nodded, but her face was too solemn. Tim knelt in front of where she sat. 'Sure?' He took her hands in his. A tear meandered down Niamh's face. Tim gently wiped it away. 'You miss him too, huh?'

She nodded. 'But it's nice to talk to someone about it.'

'Come here.' He pulled her into a hug.

Niamh buried her face in his shoulder. 'Thank you, Uncle Tim. You're a good guy.'

He kissed the side of her head. 'I'll remind you that you said so.'

She sniffed and pulled away, wiping her face with her wet sleeve. Her hand found his and squeezed.

Harriet returned with a bundle of things. She glanced at them, but didn't comment. Tim let go of Niamh's hand and stood up.

'Here y'are.' Harriet dumped the

stuff on the sofa and pulled two large towels off the top of the pile. 'Dry yourselves off.' She passed them a towel each. 'Niamh,' she said, picking out a few things from the pile, 'I've got you some of my clothes to change into. Just give me your stuff and I'll pop it in the tumble dryer.'

'Thanks.' Niamh clutched the clothes and headed into the bathroom.

Left alone with Harriet and feeling the need to do something, Tim took a corner of the towel and rubbed his wet hair. Harriet turned round and thrust something towards him, avoiding his eyes. He took it and shook out the items. It was a man's T-shirt and a pair of walking trousers.

Harriet had picked up her tea and was hurrying away.

'Are these . . . Richard's?' Tim said quietly.

Harriet stopped. 'They were.'

He looked at the clothes in his hands. 'Are you sure . . . ?'

She turned round. Her eyes were

red-rimmed and shining with tears. 'He doesn't need them now,' she said. Her gaze flicked to the clothes and then to his face. 'You may as well use them.'

Tim hesitated. These were Richard's clothes. Richard, who had broken Mel's heart. Richard, whom he'd never liked in the first place.

Harriet's eyes narrowed. 'Or you could stay in your wet clothes,' she said. 'Suit yourself.' She turned and disappeared into the kitchen.

Tim stared after her and felt like an absolute heel. She had just given him Richard's clothes. The clothes she still kept in her flat, even though their owner had been dead for a year. It must have cost her dear to hand them over to him and he'd treated them like they were soiled goods. 'Harriet, I'm — '

'Your turn, Uncle Tim.' Niamh popped out of the bathroom. She was wearing a hoodie that was too large and a pair of leggings. When he didn't move, she said, 'Bathroom's free . . . Uncle Tim. If you want to get changed . . . '

She frowned. 'What's going on?'

'Yes. Right. Of course.' He strode into the bathroom as purposefully as he could and locked himself in. The pounding of the rain was louder in here. He put the clothes on the radiator and sat on the closed toilet lid. The pub was only a few yards away. The plan had been to pick up the stuff Niamh had left and then go, but they couldn't leave Harriet alone. Not now, when she was clearly in pain. He sighed. No, he and Niamh weren't going anywhere for a while.

Careful not to aggravate his elbow, he pulled off his jumper and shirt. The shirtsleeve was speckled with blood. There was a white graze where he'd skinned his arm and his elbow was swelling a little. That would be a nasty bruise. He ran some cold water over it and hissed with the pain. There was a small cabinet in the bathroom. Should he check for a first aid kit to find a bandage? No, he couldn't rummage around a stranger's bathroom cupboards. He'd ask her later.

If not, they might have something in the shop downstairs.

He stripped off down to his underwear and picked up Richard's T-shirt. The thought of Richard immediately made him think of his sister. Mel would kill him if she knew. It was bad enough that he was lying to her about Niamh being up here to see Harriet, but if Mel ever found out that he'd been helping Harriet out, making friends with her, he would be toast. He sighed again. He was here and Mel wasn't. Niamh and Harriet needed each other right now and he wasn't going to get in the way of that. Not yet. He pulled on the T-shirt and gave a small yelp as his arm hurt.

He was a little broader and taller than Richard had been, so the sleeves ended halfway down his forearms and the trousers left his ankles exposed. He must look ridiculous, but least he was dry. He rolled up the sleeve on his bruised arm carefully.

When he went back into the living room, Harriet looked up and her expression flickered. He saw it because he was looking for it — a flash of pain and a catch in her breath. She looked away.

Niamh grinned. 'You look like your clothes shrank in the wash.'

He shrugged. 'Yeah, well. I'm a bit bigger than your dad.'

The grin died. 'Those were Dad's?' Niamh looked at Harriet.

Harriet stood up. 'I'll take those.' She took the bundle of wet clothes from him without making eye contact and disappeared into the kitchen.

Tim watched Niamh. For a moment, she looked like she was going to cry again, but her gaze flicked across to the kitchen door. There was a click and the sound of a tumble dryer starting up. Niamh took a deep breath and seemed to centre herself. She nodded and sat back down. Tim's shoulders unknotted a little. He went over and sank down next to her.

'Shit, Uncle Tim. What happened to your arm?'

Harriet put her hands on the worktop and tipped her head forward. Why had she offered these people sanctuary in her flat? They had perfectly good rooms they were paying for in the pub across the road. And Richard's clothes. It was so wrong to see them on Tim's long, gangly frame. And yet . . . she pushed herself away and contemplated her hands. And yet, it felt right. She had to let go at some point. There was a space in her chest where Richard used to be. Right now it felt enormous, but she knew how this worked. The space would shrink, slowly, until it was no longer competing with her breath. Until it was small enough to nestle down next to that other tiny emptiness and she could carry them both around with her and continue to live.

It would take time, though, and the first step was for her to go out and be a functional human being in front of her guests.

Thunder crashed outside and the roar of the downpour increased. Harriet glanced out of the tiny window of the kitchen. Oh well, it looked like Tim and Niamh were stuck here for a while. She shouted out, 'Would you two like a biscuit?'

Niamh's head popped round the door. 'What have you got?'

Harriet opened the cupboard and stared at the disorganised mess in there. Oh dear, she really had let things slide. 'Um. I don't actually have any.' She went into the living room and fetched her handbag. 'I'll just run down to the shop and get — '

'I'll go,' said Niamh. She grinned and ran off, leaving Harriet alone with Tim again. She couldn't look at him in Richard's clothes. She turned to go back into the kitchen.

'Harriet,' said Tim, 'thank you. For lending me these. It was very kind of you.'

Harriet paused and forced herself to look up. She nodded her acknowledgement and managed a little smile. Tim smiled back and there was a moment of human connection, something she hadn't felt in ages. The numbness that she had been carrying around lessened. The space in her chest suddenly felt a little easier to bear.

He moved his arm and winced. Harriet noticed that it was bleeding.

'Oh,' she said. 'You've hurt yourself. I have a first aid kit somewhere . . . ' She found it in the kitchen and returned to the living room. 'Here, let me have a look.'

'I knocked it against the dry stone wall,' he said, gingerly turning his elbow so that she could see it.

She got an alcohol wipe, put her hand on his arm to steady it and wiped the wound clean. He flinched when it first stung, but didn't make a fuss. Harriet put a clean dressing on it and tried not to think about the intimacy of being so close to someone, holding their arm. She carefully wound a short bandage around the dressing to hold it in place. Under her fingertips his skin felt warm and firm. She tied a knot on the bandage, because she had no gauze tape to stick it down. She made sure the knot was flat, and looked up. He had been looking down at what she was doing and she found herself looking straight into his eyes. His face was so close, she could feel the air move when he breathed. She couldn't look away. Her hand was still resting against his arm. Neither of them moved.

How long had it been since she'd been this close to man while sober? Hot on the heels of that thought came another. What was she doing, thinking about another man, when she should be grieving for Richard?

Footsteps thudded up the stairs, heralding Niamh's return. Harriet scrabbled away from Tim, gathering up her first aid kit.

'Just keep it dry for a bit,' she said over her shoulder.

Tim cleared his throat. 'Right. Yes. Thank you.'

9

Tim was puzzled. The Harriet who was sitting across the table from him, frowning at the Monopoly board, was a different Harriet to the one they'd found when they'd arrived only a few hours earlier. She had lost the air of frailty that she'd had, and with it, the tearfulness. At that moment, she was in the middle of a complicated discussion with Niamh about buying Leicester Square from her. She was speaking animatedly, waving her hands around, eyes shining. Niamh, it seemed, was every bit as competitive as her mother was when it came to board games. The discussion was likely to go on for a while.

Tim sat back on his dining chair and stretched, feeling the fabric of the T-shirt pull tight against him. When the rain hadn't let up, Niamh had gone down to the shop for pizza. Then they'd moved from the sofa to the small dining table in order to play a game to pass the time. He hadn't played a board game in years. He'd forgotten how absorbing it was. It was as though real life had been firmly parked outside and the only thing that mattered was what was on the board. Much to his surprise, he was enjoying himself. Maybe he needed a holiday more urgently than he'd thought.

The act of hanging out together seemed to be melting barriers. Harriet had lost some of her brittleness. Niamh was clearly happier. This was good. Agreeing to stay a few days was the right thing to have done. He thought of Mel and felt a twinge of guilt. Mel wouldn't like this.

Now that he was getting to know her, Tim had to admit that Harriet was nothing like the picture Mel had painted of her. He now knew with absolute certainty that Harriet had loved Richard. Okay, it was weird that they had such a long-distance relationship, with Richard living in Reading and coming up every two or three weekends, but it seemed to have worked for them. Harriet was, as far as he could tell, generous and kind. Now that she was coming out of her sadness, she was also quite good fun.

Harriet and Niamh came to an agreement. They shook hands. Harriet laughed. Her face lost years. She was really very attractive. Aah. No. He shouldn't be thinking that. She might be a much nicer person than he'd been lead to believe, but she was still Richard's girlfriend. Fancying her would be just . . . weird. Besides, it would be totally disloyal to Mel. This woman had broken up his sister's marriage.

'Um . . . guys, it's stopped raining.' He pointed to the window. It had actually stopped raining a while ago, but they were all having so much fun, Tim hadn't mentioned it. The view from the window was still full of grey cloud, so the respite might well only be temporary. 'We should make a dash for the pub while it's still relatively dry.'

Niamh looked down at the crowded

board, where she was clearly winning. 'We can't go now. This game is just getting interesting.' She looked back at him. 'Besides, there's nothing to DO in the pub.'

He had to admit that was true. 'It's nearly dinner time, though. We could go get something to eat.'

'Or,' said Niamh, 'we could get something to eat here. I could go down and get some more pizza from the freezer.'

Harriet, who had been watching this exchange in silence, raised her eyebrows at Niamh. Tim wondered if she wanted them to leave. She seemed to have fully recovered now, so there was no real reason to outstay their welcome. 'It's Harriet's place,' he said. 'And we've taken up far too much of her time as it is.'

'Oh, I don't mind,' said Harriet. 'It's quite nice to have company, actually. I've not been out and about as much as I normally would, and it's been . . . fun.'

Niamh shot Tim a triumphant look.

Tim said, 'Why don't you let us buy you dinner in the pub? After all you've done, it's the least I can do.'

'Please, Harriet,' said Niamh.

'In the pub?' Harriet looked dubious.

Tim remembered that she hadn't told the people in the pub about Richard's death. 'Or we could go to the bistro instead,' he said. 'They looked like they had a good menu.'

'Oh God, no. Angie would kill me if I ate at the competition,' said Harriet. 'No. The pub is fine, thank you. That would be very kind.'

⋆ ⋆ ⋆

What on earth was she going to wear? She searched through the various outfits she had. Most of her clothes were jeans and tops. She had a few smart dresses. She pulled them out and realised that she hadn't worn them in a long while. When she went out clubbing, she wore little sparkly numbers with spaghetti straps, which were perfect for a hot night club, but really weren't ideal for the pub at seven o'clock in the evening. The last time she had been to the pub for a night out had been that Christmas party where she'd got very drunk and embarrassed herself by throwing herself at Vinnie, who was going out with Angle's niece. Frank, one of the regulars from the pub, had had to carry her home. No, tonight was a night for smart, not sexy.

She pulled out an orange dress that was not too revealing. As an afterthought, she added a short black jacket. There. Smart, but not too overdressed. After she'd done her makeup, she examined her reflection. Richard's death had aged her. Even under the foundation, she could see that her complexion was less healthy. All that crying earlier had left her with puffy bags under her eyes, which didn't help.

She stood up and examined her middle. She was going out a lot less, but being in Trewton Royd, where there were hills in every direction, meant that she remained reasonably fit, thank goodness.

After a few moments' deliberation, she put her hair up, which suited her better. It was still healthy, but it needed a cut. Briefly, she wondered what Tim would think. He was, she couldn't help noticing, quite fit. He was also a terrible Monopoly player. He had no killer instinct. Unlike Niamh.

Harriet smiled at the memory. That afternoon had been the most fun she'd had in months. She liked Niamh and Tim. They seemed to have an easy way with each other. If they could recapture that relaxed atmosphere, tonight would be a good laugh, too. And that was just what she needed right now. All this time she had been trying to placate the loneliness with alcohol and meaningless encounters in nightclubs, when all she'd needed was something far simpler. Good company. A laugh.

Again, she wondered if Richard had somehow sent Naimh to her. Fanciful as it was, the thought was comforting. He was still looking out for her. Seeing Niamh was helping ease the pain. But was she meant to do something for Niamh as well? She thought of all that had been said the night before. Niamh needed to cry and talk and reconnect with memories of her father, and Harriet had helped with that. But a young girl needed her mother.

She had. In the dark, dark times after the baby had died, she tried to call her parents. Her father refused to talk to her, and her mother . . . her mother went along with her father. She had disgraced them when she eloped. There was no going back. She had written to them, but there was never a response. She wondered if they'd read her letters. Or had they just burned them on the little fire in the living room? Did they even know about their grandchild who almost existed? Did they even care?

Harriet went into the living room and looked at the phone. She reached out her hand to pick it up and punch out the number. How many times had she done this? How many times had she bottled out? The last time she'd dialled them was a few years ago, when Richard stood by her, encouraging her to at least try. Her father had hung up as soon as he realised who it was.

She curled her fingers into a fist and moved her hand back. No. It was too late for her to mend the rift between her and her own mother. But she could help with the one between Niamh and Mel.

The night before, Niamh had told her repeatedly how Mel was trying to poison her with lies about how Richard had cheated on Mel with Harriet. Richard had told his daughter that he was innocent. It wasn't strictly true. Harriet sighed. She could understand why Richard wanted to keep his daughter's view of him unsullied, but maybe he was wrong. Maybe all it was doing was hammering in the wedge between Niamh and Mel.

Harriet looked at the phone again.

She could help. Except it would be disloyal to Richard. She sighed again, picked up her handbag and let herself out of the flat.

★ ★ ★

The pub had a few regulars in already when Harriet arrived. Frank, who was in his usual seat, raised his pint glass to her and winked. Harriet winced. Memories of the Christmas party were never going to go away. Still, she had to live here and Frank was a fact of local life. She raised a hand half-heartedly. Angie finished taking a couple of food orders and beckoned Harriet to the side of the bar. Oh dear.

'Are you okay, our Harriet?' said Angie.

It was 'our Harriet' now, was it? What was that all about? 'Ye-es,' Harriet answered cautiously.

'Why didn't you tell us?' Angie's brow was furrowed when she looked up at Harriet.

'About what?'

'About your Richard. We had no idea. If we'd known . . . '

If they'd known . . . what could they have done? They couldn't have brought him back. They would have just badgered her and made her think about it when all she wanted to do was hide away and pretend it wasn't happening; that Richard was going to show up at the weekend, just like normal.

Angie laid a hand gently on Harriet's arm, all sympathy and concern. Oh Lord. She didn't want to talk about it. Not to Angie. Not to anyone. Thankfully, Niamh came into the bar and Harriet took the opportunity to escape Angie's questioning. 'Niamh.' She turned away, knowing she was being rude, but too desperate to care.

'Hi.' Niamh had changed into her spare clothes, which fit her better. Her hair was tied back, making her eyes all the more noticeable, and Harriet could see all the traces of Richard in her. Niamh grinned and Harriet automatically smiled back.

The table they had been at the night before was still free, so Harriet led her to it.

'I don't know where Uncle Tim is,' said Niamh. 'He's probably started checking his email and got distracted.' She rolled her eyes. 'He's always going on at me for being glued to my phone. He's worse.'

'What does he do?' She'd spent a whole afternoon with him and not bothered to ask. Richard had said something about Tim being an academic, but that was all she knew. She liked Tim, now that she'd got to know him, but she wasn't sure what he thought about her. Richard had said that Tim was completely under his sister's thumb. Which meant he wasn't ever going to like her. To her surprise, Harriet realised that she really wanted Tim to like her.

'He's a researcher,' said Niamh, with a trace of pride in her voice. 'He studies the effects of river pollution on freshwater fish.'

Harriet nodded and tried to think of something relevant to say. 'He must be busy.'

'I think he doesn't mind the research, but gets quite annoyed with the teaching and admin that he has to do.'

Harriet glanced across at the bar and caught Angie watching her. The landlady gave her a small smile before looking away. Harriet sighed, her earlier good mood now dented. It was silly really, to believe that she could have kept it a secret from the whole village. This place, where you could sneeze in the comfort of your bathroom and people would ask about your cold the next day. They hadn't noticed for a whole year, though. They had all assumed that Richard had dumped her and they had judged her behaviour afterwards. It wasn't great, but it was still better than having to face the fact that he was gone.

Niamh was complaining about her mother again. Harriet half-listened and made interested noises. She didn't give a monkey's about Mel, but Niamh needed her mother. An image of her own mother flashed into her mind and she was swamped by another wave of sadness. Maybe that loss wasn't as dramatic, but over time it had eroded a space in her heart, just as losing the baby and losing Richard had done.

She watched Niamh talking, a young girl trying to be a grown-up and fighting a pointless fight with her mother. Most of the things that Niamh was complaining about Harriet could do nothing about, though there was one thing she could do . . . but would Richard want her to?

'And she's always trying to make out like Dad was the bad guy. She lied about you and him, for a start. It's so pathetic that she needs to do that.' Niamh threw up her hands in indignant astonishment.

Harriet looked down. It wasn't Mel who had lied to Niamh. When they had first met, Richard hadn't told Harriet that he was still married. By the time he told her, he had filed for divorce and she was already too in love with him to send him away. Mel may not be right about the cause of the breakup of the marriage, but she was right about Richard cheating on her, even if it was only for a couple of weeks. Harriet looked up at Niamh. In letting Niamh believe her father's version of events, wasn't she in effect lying as well? Would telling Niamh the truth help heal the rift between Niamh and Mel?

She tried to focus on what Niamh was talking about instead. Niamh made a gesture with her hands to emphasize what she was saying. The mannerism was so much like Richard's that Harriet almost forgot to breathe.

How? How could he be dead? Who was she trying to kid? She couldn't deal with this. The sadness, vast and black, wrapped itself around her again.

★ ★ ★

Tim peered into the main room of the pub. Harriet was sitting at the table in the window with Niamh opposite her. Her hair was pulled up into a messy knot, highlighting the delicate lines of her face. She looked effortlessly lovely.

He was late because he had just spent twenty minutes sitting on the edge of his bed, trying to remind himself that Harriet was out of bounds. She was the woman who had broken his sister's marriage. He could not be attracted to her. Yet, when he'd come in and spotted her, his heart had lifted. He would have to be really careful to keep those sorts of feelings in check so that he didn't end up in more trouble than he already was.

It didn't take him long to see that something was wrong. He could feel it in the way Harriet was staring at the table. She had gone quiet and was nodding at what Niamh was saying, but he could tell by the way she was picking at a crack in the table top that she wasn't really focusing.

He tried to join in the conversation, but the easy atmosphere that had formed in the flat was gone now. He had rather thought she might be flirting with him earlier, but he had clearly been flattering himself. She wasn't interested in him. He should be grateful, really.

'Shall I go order the food?' he said. He pushed himself up to stand. Disappointment was putting a bit of a downer on the whole evening, but he'd promised Harriet dinner and he was going to deliver on that, even if she wasn't interested in him.

'Uncle Tim, can't I have a real drink?' Niamh said.

'No.'

'Mum lets me have a tiny bit of wine with dinner from time to time.'

He wasn't falling for that one. Now that he knew what an accomplished liar she was, he'd have to be extra careful. 'No way. I'm bending far too many rules for you as it is.' Like, every single rule Mel had set. Although she hadn't explicitly set a 'don't take her to see her Dad's mistress' rule, he was pretty sure there was one.

Niamh pulled a face. She slid out of her seat. 'You're no fun. I'm going to the loo; I'll be back in a minute.'

He watched her head off and sat back in his seat. 'I really need to get better at reading teenagers.'

'Good luck with that.' Harriet sank back into her seat, as though moving away from him. 'No one understands teenage girls. Not even teenage girls.'

'You seem to get on well with Niamh, though.' He smiled, hoping to thaw the atmosphere.

Harriet shrugged. 'She and I have something in common right now. Besides, I'm not an authority figure in her life. I'm just someone peripheral. It's not worth investing emotional energy fighting me.'

She was still being odd and formal with him, as though he were a total stranger, not someone who had sat around in her flat playing board games and making sure she didn't have a nervous breakdown. 'I'm flattered that you think I have any authority over Niamh.'

Harriet gave him a knowing look. 'You'd be surprised.'

'Why? What's she said about me?'

'You're a constant male figure in her life.' She picked up her drink. 'Whatever happens, you're always there for her and her mum. Especially when Richard . . . wasn't.'

Of course, the reason Niamh's father hadn't been a constant in her life was Harriet. The thought brought Tim back to reality. Mel was right. The warm cosiness was just an illusion. He and Harriet could never be friends. She had caused too much pain to the people he loved.

'It's not my fault, you know,' Harriet said quietly.

'Pardon?' Had he said something out loud?

She looked up. 'Mel and Richard's marriage failing. It wasn't because of me.'

As much as he liked Harriet, he couldn't let her get away with that one. 'Isn't it?' he said. 'Richard met you

157

when he was off in a sulk. He returned home and just days later, filed for divorce. I'd say there was a link there, wouldn't you?'

She narrowed her eyes. 'I didn't know he was married,' she said quietly. 'I didn't start our relationship. He did.'

He should let it go, but he just couldn't. All the evenings sitting with Mel while she cried angry tears had left a mark on him. 'But if he hadn't met you, he and Mel might have patched things up.'

Harriet gave a snort. 'Yeah. Right.'

'They might have done,' he insisted. Mel had been so sure they would. She had been so devastated when Richard walked out. 'Mel said — '

'I don't care what Mel said.' Her voice rose, attracting the attention of the people at the bar. 'I didn't ruin your sister's marriage. She did that all by herself.'

For a second, he didn't know what to say. There was a flare of doubt about Mel's version of events but the protective instinct ran it over. He opened his mouth to retort.

'This man bothering you, love?' The man from the bar appeared by the table.

Harriet shook her head. 'It's fine, Frank.'

But Frank was not to be deterred. He turned to Tim, standing over him. 'You watch what you say to her, mate. She's had some bad news lately and I'll not have you upsetting her. You got that, buddy?'

Tim nodded vigorously. He wasn't built for confrontation.

Harriet rolled her eyes. 'Thanks.'

'You're welcome, love.' He gave her a nod and ambled back to his bar stool, pausing to give Tim a warning glare.

Harriet picked up her coat. 'Listen, this was a nice idea, but I — '

'Don't go,' he said. 'I'm sorry. I shouldn't have brought that up.'

'Brought what up?' Niamh reappeared. 'What's going on?'

'Your uncle, there, called Harriet a

marriage wrecker,' said Frank from his position at the bar. 'We'll not have our Harriet upset.'

'Look,' said Harriet, 'it's fine. I'm not upset. I'm fine. All right?'

Frank gave Tim another hard stare.

Tim turned his attention to Harriet, who had stood up and was putting on her coat.

'You're not staying?' said Niamh. 'Uncle Tim?' She glared at him, again reminding him uncannily of her mother. 'What did you do?'

Tim put up his hands in protest. 'I didn't — '

'It's okay,' said Harriet. 'It's true anyway.'

Niamh spun back to glare at her. 'What is?'

Harriet drew a deep breath as though preparing herself. 'Niamh,' she said, 'there's something I need to tell you.' She reached forward and took the girl's hands. 'What your mum said is true. Your father . . . was still married to your mother when we first got together.'

160

There was a moment of stasis. Then Niamh's eyes widened. 'But you said — '

'I didn't, actually. Richard told you we met after he'd split up with Mel. I didn't have the heart to disabuse you of that. It was clearly important to Richard that you didn't think badly of him, so I just . . . didn't contradict you.'

Something in that speech was nagging at Tim. He knew what she was saying was true, but something she'd said earlier — what was it?

Niamh shook her head and wrenched her hands out of Harriet's grip. 'No. My dad wouldn't lie to me. He wouldn't.' She turned her glare on Tim. 'This is Mum's doing, isn't it? She did something. What did she make you do?'

Harriet reached forward again. 'Niamh, your dad loved you so much. He couldn't bear it if you took your mother's side and hated him. I'm sure he didn't mean for things to get out of hand — '

Niamh stepped back from her, snatching her hands out of the way. 'Get away from me. You lied to me. I thought . . . I thought you were my friend. I trusted you.' Tears filled her eyes. 'I . . . I hate you.' She turned and ran out of the room.

'Niamh!' Tim noted with gratitude that she'd gone upstairs, rather than out into the night. He wanted to go after her, but first he turned to Harriet. 'I'm sorry,' he said. 'I didn't mean to — '

'Best go speak to her,' said Harriet wearily. She turned, gave Frank at the bar a wave, and left. Tim watched her go, his thoughts too scattered for him to react.

10

Harriet walked briskly across to the flat and locked herself in. The room swam beyond her tears. 'I'm sorry, Richard,' she said to the silence of the flat. 'I know you wanted to keep the image of you that Niamh had, but it was doing so much harm. Niamh needs Mel more than ever, now that you're . . . ' She swallowed through the tightness in her throat. 'Now that you're gone.'

The silence remained unfeeling. She took in the dining table, drawn away from its usual place in the corner so that they could play Monopoly, and the three mugs on the side. The place looked more lived-in than it had done for months. Harriet shrugged off her jacket and set about tidying up. It had been a fun afternoon. When was the last time she'd had fun? Just because Richard was lost to her didn't mean she couldn't carry on living. She had been here before, when existence was a battle, and she had got through it. The cold spaces in her chest jostled against each other. She would just have to hold on to them both and get her life back on track. For their sakes as well as hers.

Niamh coming to see her had been a blessing. Harrier had rather hoped that she could remain in contact with her, not least to see her grow up into a woman that Richard would have been proud of. But it didn't seem likely now. Niamh had opened her heart to Harriet and Harriet had lied to her. Regardless of her motives, Niamh wouldn't see past that. Tim wouldn't encourage her to, anyway. Harriet had to admit a hint of disappointment at Tim. She had liked him. He was nice. But his blind loyalty to his sister was more extreme than she'd expected. Shame. He was rather cute, too.

She chided herself. Cute was dangerous. She couldn't cheat on Richard. Especially not with evil Mel's brother.

She sighed and got to work.

Once the flat had been restored to order, she set her laptop on the table and pulled up her client list. A lot of them had stopped contacting her because she had turned down so much work from them. She hadn't meant to turn it down. It had just happened. Responding to messages felt so difficult, she'd left it, until people took her silence to mean she wasn't interested, and eventually all communication had ceased.

The first thing to do would be to get back in touch. Maybe explain that it had been a year of difficult circumstances. Get back on their radar. She rubbed her fingers together while she thought it through. Then began to type.

* * *

Tim had been standing outside Niamh's door for five minutes, debating whether to knock. Finally he did. 'Niamh,' he said to the door, 'can I talk to you?'

'Go away.'

'Niamh, honey, I know you're upset, but . . . well, it might help to talk to someone.'

There was silence from the other side of the door for a few seconds, then shuffling and the door opened. A mascara-streaked Niamh stood there, looking so very young that Tim's heart squeezed. 'Can I come in?' he asked.

Instead of replying, she shuffled out of the way. The room was small, and cramped now that two people were in it. Tim sat down on the bed. Niamh shut the door and sat down beside him.

Now that he was here, Tim was at a loss as to where to start. 'You okay?' he said.

Niamh sniffed and shook her head. 'Why would Dad lie to me?'

Tim took a breath and exhaled slowly. 'Well,' he said, feeling his way to the end of the sentence, 'I think he just wanted you to think well of him. Whatever his other faults, he did love you. Even I could see that. And you adored him. Put him on a bit of a pedestal. If . . . if it were me . . . I would do anything I had to in order to make sure I stayed on that pedestal.'

Niamh said nothing. Her eyes filled with tears again.

He knew what he had to say. He felt disloyal saying it, but it had to be done. 'Your mother can be a bit . . . well, she was very upset about the fact that your dad wanted to divorce her. And when she's upset, she can be very harsh. I'm guessing Richard was worried that she might be trying to influence how you felt about him.'

'I don't understand. What are you saying, Uncle Tim?'

Ugh. This was more difficult than he'd expected. 'Harriet had a point. She didn't break up their marriage. It was already broken. Your parents tried couples' counselling and all sorts of things. Richard wanted a divorce, but your mum didn't. Richard stormed out of the house one night saying he needed some time to think. He didn't tell us where he was going. Your mum was left alone, with you.'

'You came to stay with us,' said Niamh. 'I remember. Mum was in a foul mood. You took me to the cinema, like, three days in a row or something.'

'That's right.' His heart broke at the thought of that little nine-year-old who was already old enough to know something was wrong. 'Anyway, it turned out Richard had rented a cottage in the middle of nowhere. Well, here. And while he was staying here, gathering his thoughts . . .'

'He met Harriet.'

'Yes. He moved his stuff out and filed for divorce the following week.'

Niamh pulled her knees up to her chest and rested her chin on them. 'But why would Harriet lie to me?'

Tim shrugged. 'Who knows? I'm guessing your mum isn't Harriet's favourite person, so there's no reason for her to correct something that makes your mum look bad.' He had to admit that Harriet seemed like a nicer human being than that. 'And she loved your dad. She maybe wanted to keep that memory clean.'

Niamh made a noncommittal noise in her throat. After a moment of silence, she said, 'She really did love him, didn't she?'

He thought of the grief they'd witnessed and the clothes lovingly kept. 'Yes, I think she really did.'

'And he loved her. He always got this goofy look on his face whenever he talked about her.' Niamh made a vague gesture around her face. 'It was puke-inducing, really. But sweet, y'know.'

Tim nodded. Harriet was probably a much more fun person to be around than Mel. The guilty feeling worsened. He shouldn't be disloyal to his sister. But then again, it was true.

'Why did Harriet tell me the truth just now? Why not let me go on believing that Mum was wrong and Dad was a saint? I don't understand.'

He shifted his weight a little. 'Perhaps, now that she's got to know you, she values you too highly to keep lying

to you.' He sighed. 'People are complicated, Niamh. Life is messy. Sometimes,
as much as you'd like there to be a
clear-cut right and wrong way to do
things, there isn't. Sometimes . . . ' He
threw his hands up, no longer sure what
to say. 'Sometimes shit happens.'

This elicited a small smile. 'Like what
happened with you with Sarah-the-
bitch and your back-stabbing friend?'

'How'd you know about that?' He
was pretty sure he hadn't told her. They
hadn't seen much of each other since
then.

'Mum.'

Obviously. 'Of course. Well, yes. A bit
like Sarah and Nick, I suppose.' He
rubbed his face. 'Although Sarah said
she split up with me before she started
seeing Nick.'

'Do you believe her?'

He didn't want to believe her. It was
easier to be hurt and angry when you
felt you had a very good reason to be.
He thought back to the weeks before
Sarah dumped him. She had been

acting more and more distant, and Nick had been avoiding him. But then, if you realised you fancied your best mate's girlfriend, you *would* avoid them, wouldn't you?

'Uncle Tim?' Niamh was frowning, her mascara-streaked face looking comically concerned.

'Y-yes. I think I do believe her.' When he stopped to think about it, neither Sarah nor Nick was the sort of person to sneak around behind his back. Why had he even thought that? He realised with a start that every time he'd come close to analysing it before, Mel had charged in and told him he would be an idiot to forgive them. She had been furious on his behalf.

Dear God. Was he such a hopeless case that he took all his opinions from his sister? No. He just wanted a quiet life, so he took the easiest option. With Mel, that was always to agree with her. Even if he didn't, really. He'd been so tired and miserable that he'd forgotten he was only humouring her.

He looked across at Niamh, who was here in a pub in the middle of nowhere because of him. She'd tried to tell him what was wrong, but he'd been too taken with Mel's opinions to listen. It had to stop. He had to look out for Niamh. If that meant standing up to Mel from time to time, then he'd have to learn to do that.

'I think Sarah would rather be straight with me and hurt me than try and sneak around behind my back in order to keep me happy.'

Niamh nodded. 'So are you still friends with either of them?'

'No. Although, now that I've spoken to you, I'm starting to think I should get over myself and make peace.'

She gave him a smile. 'I think you should.'

'I think I will.'

Niamh suddenly put her arms around him and gave him a squeeze. 'Thank you, Uncle Tim.'

He hugged her back, his throat tightening with emotion. 'What for, darling?'

'For coming after me. For being cool about me being such a halfwit. For letting me talk to Harriet.' She released him and wiped her cheek with the heel of her hand. 'Mum would never have done that. She'd have just gone apeshit at me.'

'She means well,' said Tim. 'She's ... having a difficult time at the moment.'

Niamh went over to the table and found a tissue. 'I should be nicer to her, I guess.'

'Well, it wouldn't hurt.'

They chatted a little while longer until Niamh started to yawn. Tim left her to get ready for bed and went back to his room. He felt more optimistic about Niamh than he had done for ages. It was a shame she had to find out about Richard's lies, but perhaps the realisation that her father wasn't the perfect man she'd built him up to be would make her mellow a little towards her mother. If that happened, then something good would have come from this whole adventure.

He kicked off his shoes and stretched out on the bed. It was nice of Harriet to give Niamh so much time and attention. Granted, their interaction seemed to help Harriet as well, but still. It was nice of her. He should thank her. And apologise for what happened downstairs. He had all but accused her of being a marriage breaker . . . come to think of it, he *had* accused her of being a marriage breaker. Tim closed his eyes and groaned.

It wasn't entirely clear to him why she'd told Niamh about Richard lying, though. He frowned. That thing that was nagging at the back of his mind suddenly came into focus. *I didn't know*, she'd said. She hadn't known that Richard was married when they met. When had she found out?

He sat up. They would be going home tomorrow and that would be the last he saw of this little village and of Harriet. He couldn't leave things the way they were. He had to apologise to her for a start. Putting his shoes back on again, he locked his door and headed out of the pub.

The view caught him by surprise again. The sky had cleared since the rain and was now peppered with stars. As he walked away from the lights of the pub, there seemed to be more and more stars appearing. He stopped at the end of the path and looked across the road. The light was on in Harriet's apartment. Good.

11

Sitting on the sofa with her laptop on her knees, Harriet pressed send and crossed another name off her list. It was going to be difficult building up momentum again, but hopefully the fact that she had done good work for them in the past would encourage some of her old clients to come back.

As she leaned across to pick up her coffee, a message pinged in. Drink forgotten, she opened it. It was from one of the people she'd emailed. It read, 'Glad you're better now. I will certainly bear you in mind when I next need some work doing. Take care of yourself.'

She dashed off a quick reply. People were responding. Phew. Slowly, she was coming back. Harriet closed the lid of the laptop and rubbed her eyes. It felt good, this reconnecting. She had lost a year, but it was okay. She could salvage things and start to live again. All thanks to Niamh and Tim. In a less than twenty-four hours, they had undone months of damage.

Harriet picked up her coffee and found that it had gone cold. Never mind. She fancied a glass of wine. She stood up, then sat back down again. The drinking needed to stop, too. That would be the first outward sign of her recovery. But not tonight. She felt too bruised and fragile to go without. She'd only had one glass so far, she reasoned. Another wouldn't be too much.

Putting the laptop on the floor, she hunted down the half-sized bottle of white that she had in the fridge and poured herself a glass. She took the photo of herself and Richard off the fridge and took it into the living room with her. He wasn't coming back. The best thing she could do for him now was to ride her ocean of sadness until she found somewhere to stand again. She touched his face in the picture and wondered yet again if he had somehow sent Niamh and Tim to her. She could see why he might have sent Niamh, but why Tim?

Harriet took a sip of wine, wincing at the cold. Tim. After the little spat they had in the pub, she wasn't sure how she felt about him. He seemed to have done nothing but bumble around since he'd got there, but all of it had been well meant and all of it, in one way or another, had helped. She thought of his face when he'd upset her. He had looked mortified. Harriet smiled. He was . . . sweet. She recalled the sight of him in Richard's T-shirt that was too small for him. He had muscles in all the right places, too.

For a mad minute she wondered what it would feel like to be pressed against him. Then she remembered that he was Richard's ex-brother-in-law. Mel would be so angry if Harriet managed to seduce Tim. The idea made her smile.

She shook her head. No, Tim was out

of bounds. Maybe if they'd met under different circumstances . . . It had been so long since she'd looked at the world clearly that it was possible that any man would look attractive right now. Anyway, he would be gone by tomorrow after-noon and she wouldn't see him again. She'd try and keep in touch with Niamh, but she had no reason to keep any links with Tim.

She settled back down on the sofa and pulled the laptop onto her knees again. The bell rang. Someone was at the door. Frowning, Harriet got back up again. She opened the window that faced the side street and leaned out to see who it was. Tim stood outside with no coat on, fidgeting to keep warm. What kind of a numpty went out with-out a coat in the middle of the night?

'Oh,' said Harriet, 'it's you. What do you want?'

He looked up. 'Er, hi. Can I talk to you? I'd like to apologise.'

She felt a rush of pleasure that he'd come to look for her. But there was no sense in making things easy for him.

She gave an exaggerated sigh. 'You may as well come in. Everyone in this village thinks I'm some sort of marriage-wrecking floozie now anyway.'

He started to say something, but she cut him off by shutting the window. She padded downstairs and let him in. 'Go on up,' she said. She shut the door and went upstairs herself.

He was standing in her living room. 'Look, I'm sorry about — '

She waved the apology aside. 'It's okay.' She plugged her laptop in to charge. 'How's Niamh doing?'

'She's all right, actually. She was upset to start with, but I think she'll be okay. We had a chat. She knows her dad loved her.' He rubbed his arm absently, just above the bandage.

A voice in Harriet's head observed that he had nice forearms. Reminding herself that she had to keep her distance from him, she picked up her wine. 'I didn't know if it was the right thing to tell her. It was important to Richard that she thought well of him.'

'But she had him on an impossible pedestal,' Tim said.

She shrugged. Richard wasn't going to do anything now that would push him off his pedestal. He could have stayed there for all time, now that he was gone. 'That's not why I told her.'

She pulled out one of the dining chairs and sat down. Tim joined her at the opposite side of the table. The room felt a little bigger now that there was a table in between them.

He leaned against the table with his good arm. 'Why did you tell her, then?'

'Niamh's lost her father. She needs her mother more than ever. I didn't want her to think that her mum was being a complete bitch and making things up to sully Richard's memory.' Harriet tapped a fingernail against her glass. What kind of person risked hurting their child just to get revenge on the child's father? She disliked Mel intensely. 'But Mel doesn't exactly help herself with her attitude. Poor Niamh shouldn't have to come and find a relative stranger to help her grieve. Her mum should be there for her.'

'Mel did her best.' Of course he jumped in to defend his precious sister.

Harriet rolled her eyes. 'Oh yes, counselling. You said. It's not like you talk about it a few times and then BAM, grief over. It doesn't work like that.'

Tim sighed and suddenly looked very tired. 'I know. I know. You're right. It's my fault. I should — '

'No, Tim, it's not your fault. It's Mel's. Why do you always defend that woman? She's self-centred and controlling and thoughtless. What power does she have that makes you think you have to look after her all the time?'

Tim inhaled sharply. He looked like he'd been slapped. He blinked and looked down at his hands, frowning. Harriet felt a stir of unease. She'd hit a nerve. Seconds passed. When he still didn't reply to her, she felt even worse. She'd just shot her mouth off. Clearly there was more to this than she realised. 'I'm sorry,' she said. 'That was out of order.'

He put up a hand to stop her, but didn't look up. 'It's okay,' he said. 'You have a point.' He finally dragged his gaze up to meet hers and she was surprised to see pain in his expression. 'Mel's my twin. When we were children, Mel was ill. A lot. She had childhood leukaemia and we thought she was going to die.'

Harriet's hand rose to her mouth. Ouch. In light of this information, what she'd just said was incredibly insensitive. 'I'm so sorry.'

He carried on speaking, as though he hadn't heard. 'For a while, our whole life was hospitals and treatment regimes and . . . and everything focused on Mel. The treatment worked and eventually Mel got better, but I guess we never stopped focusing on her. The slightest thing and it was back to hospital for tests. Even after we grew up and moved away from home, I kinda stuck around to make sure she was okay. I know Mel can be self-centred and demanding, but it's because we made her like that. So, in a way, it is my fault.'

Suddenly, other things Richard had said made sense. About how Mel needed to get her own way. About how she couldn't stand Richard giving baby Niamh too much attention. At the time Harriet had dismissed the idea of a woman being jealous of her own child as ridiculous . . . but it turned out, again, that she didn't have a clue. What did she know about motherhood? She'd never got that far.

She reached across the table to Tim and touched his arm. He started.

She moved her hand back. 'I'm sorry. I jumped to conclusions. I really must stop doing that.' She gave him what she hoped was an apologetic smile.

He blinked, but didn't smile. 'You're a nice person,' he said. 'What you did for Niamh — you know, going to get her. Making sure she was safe. That was kind.'

'Not especially. The poor child was frantic when she called. Anyone else would have done the same.'

'But telling her the truth about Richard, even though it made you look bad . . . that was something special.'

His gaze met hers. His eyes were blue. A surprising deep blue.

'I can see why Richard liked you.'

It was the first complimentary thing he'd said to her. She felt a small flush of warmth somewhere in her belly. 'Thank you.'

He continued looking at her, as though seeing her properly for the first time. She fought down the urge to smooth her hair with her hands. He frowned.

'What?' she asked.

'You said you didn't know . . . Earlier, in the pub, you said you didn't know that Richard was married.'

Oh. So that was why he was looking at her. He was trying to figure out when she'd found out about Richard's lies. Not any other reason. She surprised herself by feeling a bump of disappointment. She must like him more than she'd thought.

'Yes. At first, I didn't know.' She looked up at him. 'I'm not the sort of person who goes around breaking up other people's marriages, honestly. Christ, I know how hard it is — ' But he didn't need telling. He'd watched his sister's marriage fall apart, twice, by the sound of things. She cleared her throat. Keep to the subject. 'Richard told me that he wasn't with his wife anymore. I took that to mean he was divorced. But obviously . . . shades of grey.' She took a large gulp of wine.

She had met Richard and her world had gone from black and white to technicolour. Falling in love had happened instantly, with no preamble. That glorious, breathless summer. She thought of that summer now and it seemed a little more distant. A little less vivid. 'He . . . we were together for a week and he had to go. He texted me and called me every day. And then, about four days after he'd gone back, he called me and told me he hadn't been entirely honest. He said that he had only now left his wife.'

Tim's gaze was fixed on her. 'And you didn't mind?'

Harriet gave a little laugh. 'Oh, I minded. I was most unhappy. I think I swore rather a lot and I hung up on him. But then the world seemed suddenly so very drab, I couldn't bear it. In the end I decided that knowing that he'd once lied to me and then come clean about it was not as bad as knowing that I'd had a chance at something wonderful and let it slip through my fingers.' She shrugged one shoulder. 'I guess you don't choose how you fall in love. Sometimes it's not perfect, but then, what is?'

For a moment, Tim said nothing. He seemed to be thinking this through, turning the concept over. Finally, he said, 'That's very generous of you.'

It was. But it was also entirely the opposite. Generosity involved giving something away while you still had use for it. All she had done was to keep him, which was what she'd desperately wanted to do in the first place.

'I'm a generous person,' she said. She looked down at her glass, now nearly empty. She couldn't offer Tim a drink, because there was hardly a glassful left. Maybe coffee? Partway through this thought, she realised that she didn't want him to leave. Not yet. She had missed this. Company. Companionship. She lived in a village full of people, yet she'd chosen to make herself lonely. It hadn't been a conscious choice. It had just happened. She was only realising it now, as though she was waking up.

'Would you like a drink?'

Tim glanced at the wine.

'I meant coffee, or tea. I don't have any wine left, sorry.'

'I was just going to say, I'm not really a white wine drinker.' He smiled, making his face light up. 'Coffee would be lovely. Thank you.'

★ ★ ★

Tim looked out of the window at the quiet street outside. Nothing moved. Nothing. For someone like him, who had grown up in the city and got used to watching the passing headlights sweep across the ceiling while he fell asleep, it might as well have been on another planet. Glancing up, he saw the stars. So many more than he was used to seeing. He tried to picture living here all the time, in a place where the stars shone so bright.

And Harriet. The more he got to know her, the brighter she became. There was something about her, a barely contained energy that was out of place in this sleepy village. She came out of the kitchen, the light catching her hair and making her glow. For a fleeting instant he wondered what it would be like to kiss her. What was wrong with him?

She came up and handed him his drink.

'Can I ask a question?' Tim said.

'Sure.'

'Why here? You said you moved here,

but you didn't grow up here. You work online, so you could have moved down to be with Richard, but you chose to stay here. Why?'

She gestured to the window. 'Look at it,' she said. 'When the sun's out and the birds are singing, there's nowhere so beautiful.'

He looked and saw stars and dark hillsides rising up either side of the village. He had seen it in the daytime and thought it beautiful. Now, in the velvet night, it looked altogether too quiet.

She came to stand next to him, so close that there was barely a gap between their shoulders. 'See those houses over there?' She gestured towards a distant glow at the top of a hill. 'That's the new housing development. Richard looked at a house there. He was going to buy it and I was going to live in it. But . . . ' She turned back and faced the flat. 'But I didn't want to. This . . . ' She waved her glass to sweep the living room. 'This is mine. I can afford the rent on it. It's my home. I didn't want to leave it.' She smiled. 'So we abandoned that plan. He was only ever up here at the weekends anyway. He had to stay near Niamh.'

Tim turned around too and looked at the flat properly. It was small, he'd noticed that from the start, but it was homely. It looked more lived-in than his sparsely furnished place.

'You never considered moving down?'

An odd looked flashed across her face. She shook her head. 'No. I lived in London once. When I was . . . oh, too young. And stupid. When I came here, I wanted to get as far away from London as I could and . . . ' She took a sip from her drink, slowly, as though buying herself time. 'Well, can you think of another place less like London than this?' When she moved her hand down, it trembled.

Tim stared at her and sensed something enormous behind her decision to leave London. 'What happened?' he said softly.

She glanced at him sideways and said nothing.

'You don't have to tell me,' he said. 'I didn't mean to pry. I'm sorry.'

She blinked slowly. 'No, it's okay.' She sighed and leaned against the windowsill. 'I grew up on the other side of the Pennines. Not far from here, but far enough.' Her mouth twisted into a bitter half smile. 'I left home young. Very young. I met a man . . . well, he was almost still a boy, really. Geoff. He was nineteen and I was seventeen. My parents were very . . . well, they would never have let me do it . . . so we ran away. My parents disowned me. We were so sure of ourselves. So stupid.'

She put down her mug. 'We thought we were happy. Then I got pregnant, and he realised he wasn't so happy after all. The baby . . . ' Her voice sounded thin and distant. Her hand curled into a fist and rested against her side. 'The baby went. And a few weeks later, he went too. He moved to Spain and got a job running a bar. I was left with nothing. No baby, no boyfriend, just a bedsit I couldn't afford to rent and this huge, huge sadness.' She was staring into the middle distance now. Her hand unclenched and dropped limp at her side.

'Oh, Harriet.' He didn't know what to say. She had lost so much, and now she'd lost Richard too. He wanted to reach out, put an arm around her, comfort her, but he couldn't. Could he? He moved a hand tentatively in her direction.

Harriet drew in a sharp breath. 'Anyway,' she said, snapping back into the present. 'I survived. I moved to a shared house. Worked as a temp in an office for a few years. Did copywriting by night until I had enough clients to be self-reliant. As soon as I could afford to, I came back up North. I couldn't go see my parents, obviously, but it's cheaper up here. And nicer.'

Tim moved his hand back. She clearly wasn't going to appreciate a hug. He had been a sounding board for Mel's anger and for Niamh's confusion. He had been able to comfort them by being there. But this was new to him. He could hear the pain in her voice, see it in the tremor of her fingers. But she didn't want comforting. She definitely didn't want his sympathy. 'It is nice here,' he said carefully. 'Lots of . . . sky.'

Harriet gave him a small smile. 'This flat was a little more expensive than the other places I'd looked at, but when I got here, I went for a walk around the village . . . and I had the strangest feeling that the place had been waiting for me to come and find it. Like I belonged here.' She put her head to one side and a small smile pulled at her lips. 'I met Richard within half an hour of that and then I knew. This was where I was meant to be.'

Her gaze rose to a photo of her and Richard framed on the mantelpiece. There was a small white feather stuck onto the frame. She swallowed, muscles moving on her elegant neck. 'Richard's not here now . . . but I think I still belong here. I just forgot to look around properly for a while.'

There was a lump in Tim's throat. Here he was, carrying around a stupid grudge that belonged to his sister, when this woman was dealing with so much grief. Old grief. New grief. So much sadness. 'I'm sorry. It must be hard dealing with Richard's death all alone.'

'Oh, I'll be okay. Now that people know, they'll be supportive. They may be nosy and annoying, but they look out for me, just as I'd always look out for them.' Harriet's smile warmed. 'I can't believe I'd forgotten that until Frank reminded me this evening.' She reached behind him and pulled the curtain shut.

He smiled back. 'I'm really sorry about what happened in the pub, by the way. I didn't mean to sound like I was accusing you. I — '

She laughed softly and moved away. 'Don't worry about it. It's not exactly unjustified anyway.'

He raised his eyebrows over his mug.

She shrugged. 'Since Richard died . . . sometimes, when I have a drink, I get so desolate. I need someone to hold me. It gets so bad, that need. Sometimes I go into town, go clubbing, just to have some contact with someone . . . anyone.' She looked straight at him, chin raised, defying him to judge her.

'Oh.' Tim spoke without thinking. 'I know exactly how that feels.' He realised what he'd just said and felt the blood rise in his face. He looked up. Harriet was looking at him. Her gaze met his. The texture of the air changed. His heart kicked up a notch. He should say something to break the tension, but he couldn't take his gaze off her lips.

Harriet very deliberately put her mug down on the table and took a couple of steps towards him. Tim's heart thundered in his ears. His body, of its own accord, moved to meet her. He took her face in his hands and kissed her.

She tasted of wine and coffee. He forgot everything else and gave himself up to the moment. Her mouth against his. The press of her breasts against his chest, the thrill of her fingertips in his hair. He pulled her closer and her legs brushed against his thighs. It had been so long and she felt so soft . . . so good.

It was only when she pulled away so that she could unbutton his shirt that rational thought intruded. Niamh was in the pub across the road. She was safe, but what would she think? He couldn't risk upsetting her by making her life more complicated than it already was. And Mel. Mel would be furious with him. As much as he wanted this, he had to think about his sister and niece first. His sleeping with Richard's ex would never be a good thing for either of them. He caught Harriet's hands in his and moved them away.

She looked up, the fire in her eyes dimming under a frown. 'What's wrong?'

Oh, he wanted to carry on kissing her. But he had to be strong. 'This is a bad idea,' he said. 'You're Richard's — ' Richard's what? Widow? Ex? He wasn't sure what to call her. 'Richard's . . . '

She stepped back as though he'd stung her, wrapped her arms around herself. 'I'm not Richard's,' she said quietly. 'I'm not anybody's. I'm mine.'

'Harriet, I'm so sorry.' He reached towards her, but stopped when she flinched away from him. 'I'm sorry. It's me. I'm just — '

She shook her head, not meeting his eyes. 'You're right. It's a bad idea. You should go.' Without looking at him, she opened the door for him. 'If you pull the main door to behind you, it should lock itself.'

Tim nodded. 'I'll message you in the morning, before we go.'

Harriet didn't reply.

He had hurt her. He wanted to touch her, give her a hug, but he couldn't trust himself anymore. 'I'm sorry, Harriet,' he said, again. 'Good night.'

Her silence followed him all the way down the stairs and out into the cold, empty street.

12

She wasn't going to go over there. Harriet could see the pub though the window of the shop as she slapped the sign round to 'open'. Tim had messaged her to say they were leaving after breakfast. She wanted to go and say goodbye to Niamh. To say, *Please don't hate me.* But that would mean seeing Tim, and she couldn't face that. She hauled the newspapers onto the counter and sorted them. It wasn't that she was embarrassed about kissing him. Well, maybe a bit. It was all very well getting your tongue down a random horny stranger in a nightclub, but when it was someone you knew, someone you actually wanted to see again . . . that was different. And stupid. She should have left well alone.

'Idiot,' she muttered as she stacked the papers neatly in the display. The remaining pile was for the pub. She normally waited until Ellie, the assistant from the bakery, came in with the loaves and cinnamon rolls, and got her to mind the shop while she ran across with the papers. Maybe this time she could ask Ellie to take the papers instead.

Harriet rubbed a hand over her face. This was new. This discomfort. It twanged inside her, resonating in time to the sadness that she carried around with her. Kissing any number of random men in nightclubs had never made her feel like this. They were strangers who served a purpose. By the next day they were irrelevant. Like a bottle of wine. You drank it. Paid for it with a hangover the next day, then forgot about it. You didn't have to feel guilty for drinking it. Yet kissing Tim had been different.

She knew him. She *liked* him. Harriet sighed. If she was being honest, she fancied him and ever since she found out about his childhood, she felt like she understood him. If it hadn't been for that, she wouldn't have told him about all that other stuff. She pressed a fist against her chest and rubbed at the parcel of emptiness she carried there. Richard and the baby who never even had a name.

She got the pricing gun to mark up the new stock. If Niamh and Tim hadn't shown up, she would still have been wearing her grief like a cloak, pushing away the very people who would help her. She should go and say goodbye. It would be awkward, but she only had to get through this one encounter with Tim. She'd never see him again.

By the time Ellie arrived, bringing with her the smell of cinnamon and sugar, Harriet had made up her mind. She quickly explained that she was nipping across to the pub, grabbed the parcel of newspapers, and hurried off before she talked herself out of it.

Niamh was standing at the bar, watching Angie wrap up a round of sandwiches. She turned when Harriet showed up. 'Hi.'

'Hi,' said Harriet. 'Are you . . . still talking to me?'

Niamh nodded. 'Uncle Tim explained.'

'Don't judge Richard too harshly. Or me.'

Niamh flung her arms around Harriet and squeezed her. 'I don't,' she said, her voice muffled in Harriet's shoulder. 'I'm so glad I came to see you. I feel like . . . like I've got to know Dad again. All the good stuff, you know. I need to hold on to the good stuff and remember it.' She let go of Harriet and took a step back. There were tears in her eyes. 'You helped me remember.'

Tears rose in Harriet's eyes as well. 'You helped me too.'

They hugged each other again, less fiercely this time.

'Keep in touch, yeah?' said Harriet. 'If you ever want to chat, you know where to find me.'

'I will,' said Niamh. Her eyes flicked to someone behind Harriet.

Harriet didn't have to turn to know

that Tim had come downstairs. She turned anyway.

Bags lined his eyes. He hadn't bothered to shave, giving him a rough dusting of stubble. It suited him. Less professor, more Indiana Jones. 'You came,' he said.

'Well, I couldn't let you run off without saying goodbye.' For a second, they stood there, not sure what to do next. Finally, Harriet stuck out her hand. 'Well, goodbye, Tim. It was really nice to meet you.'

He shook her hand, his warm fingers wrapping around her hand. She had a sudden memory of those hands cupping her face and felt a flash of heat. His eyes widened and he dropped her hand.

'It was nice to meet you too,' he said, sounding very formal. 'Thank you so much for all you've done for Niamh. I don't dare think how things would have gone if you hadn't got her from the station.'

'It's fine. I'm glad to be able to help.'

Tim looked past her at Niamh. 'Ready?'

Niamh waved the packet of sandwiches. 'Ready.' She stepped up to Harriet and gave her another hug. 'I'll message you,' she said.

'You do that.' Harriet smiled and looked into Niamh's eyes, which reminded her so much of Richard's. 'Be . . . ' She had been about to say 'be careful', but Niamh would have been hearing that far too much. 'Be kind to yourself,' she said instead.

'I will.' Niamh gave her a kiss on the cheek. 'Bye, Harriet.' She turned to her uncle. 'Come on then, Uncle Tim. Let's get this show on the road.'

Tim rolled his eyes. 'Thank you,' he called out to Angie. He gave Harriet a small wave and turned to leave.

'Don't forget to rate us on TripAdvisor.' Typical Angie.

Harriet said, 'Look after yourself, Tim.'

He paused and looked over his shoulder. His eyes, such startling blue, looked into hers and she felt a desperate urge to grab onto him and beg him not to leave. 'You too,' he said, softly.

She and Angie trailed after them to the door and watched them leave.

'Well, they were nice,' said Angie. 'Especially that Tim.'

Harriet tensed, sensing where this was going.

'Went out for a walk late last night, he did,' said Angie.

'Did he, now?' said Harriet.

'Yes. He was gone ever such a while.'

'Must have been a long walk, then.' Harriet rubbed her hands together. 'Right. I'd better get back to the shop. See you later, Ange.'

'Harriet — ' Angie's voice dropped to a more conspiratorial pitch.

Harriet narrowed her eyes. She would talk about it, but not yet. 'Angie . . . ?' she said, a note of warning in her voice.

Angie caught her gaze and sighed. 'Nothing. You know where to find me if you need me. I'll see you later, love.'

Harriet nodded. She left the pub car park and paused. From here, she could still see Tim's car, crawling up the hill on its way out of the village. To the other side was the church and beyond it the patchwork of rippling green. Harriet breathed it in. Tim had asked her why she'd chosen here, of all places. She let out her breath and smiled. Because it felt like home.

* * *

The hill out of the village was so steep that Tim's car was complaining, even in second gear. He shifted down to first. They crested the hill and he shifted gears with a little huff of relief. In his pocket, his phone connected to the network and buzzed. Work messages, no doubt. They would have to wait until he got home, just like the emails in his inbox. He'd glanced through them that morning and decided none of them were urgent enough to ruin these last few hours of tranquillity. He felt like he'd been away from work for weeks. Really, it had only been two days. In front of him the road, hemmed by drystone walls, wound through fields. It was a different world to the one he knew. He shifted his shoulders a little and was surprised at how loose they felt. The tension that he'd been carrying around with him ever since he'd found out that Niamh had run away was finally abating. He was taking Niamh home.

They just had to make it back down to the house before Mel and Alex got home and everything would be fine. Niamh was happier. He and Niamh were friends again and Mel need never know.

Niamh's phone was buzzing madly too. She pulled it out and stared at the screen. 'Huh? Weird.'

'What's up?'

'I've got fifteen missed calls. They're all from the same number. It's not someone on my contacts list.'

'Did they leave a message?'

Niamh nodded. She fiddled about for a minute, then held the phone to her ear. Tim could hear the voicemail kicking in. The first message burst out, a babble of angry invective. Niamh's eyes widened. She looked across at Tim, horror writ large on her face.

He didn't know to ask who it was. It was Mel.

'She knows,' said Niamh. 'She knows where we are!'

'But how? How can she possibly know? We haven't told anyone.'

'She's been tracking my phone.' Niamh's face was bloodless. 'Oh Uncle Tim, she's going to kill me.'

'Shit,' said Tim. 'She's going to kill us both.'

13

Several hours later, Tim pulled up outside Mel's house. Alex's car was already in the drive. Mel had come back early when she realised what was going on. He turned the engine off and looked at Niamh. Poor kid, she had no colour in her cheeks at all.

'Ready?' he said.

'No.' She sank in her seat. 'Oh God, I'm going to die.'

Tim sighed. 'You and me both. I guess waiting out here until she notices the car is probably not a good idea. We'd best get it over with.'

'It's okay for you, you get to go home. I have to live with it.'

'Might have been an idea to think about that before you ran away,' he said, rather more sharply than he'd intended.

Niamh sank even further into her seat.

His shoulders were knots of pain and he had a headache. He rubbed his forehead. Snapping at Niamh wasn't going to help anyone. 'I'm sorry, Niamh,' he said. 'I'll do my best to help, but we really are going to have to face your mum at some point. Let's just do it.' He opened his car door. 'Come on.'

He had to go around to her side and open the door to get her to come out. He fetched her bag and they trailed reluctantly to the front door. When Niamh put her key in the lock, there was a flurry of movement and Mel wrenched the door open. The first thing she did was to grab Niamh to her in a fierce hug.

'Oh, thank goodness, you're okay,' said Mel.

Niamh glanced over her shoulder at Tim. 'Of course I'm okay. Mum, I texted you, like, ten minutes ago.'

'Don't give me that attitude, young lady,' she said, motherly concern turning stern. 'You owe me an explanation.' She let go of her daughter and glared at Tim. 'As for you.' She levelled a finger at him. 'What the hell were you thinking?'

Her fury blazed at him through her eyes. Tim held up his hands. Behind Mel, Niamh was giving him a meaningful look as though reminding him to stick to the story. Like he needed reminding.

'She was with me the whole time,' he said. 'Perfectly safe. We just went away for a day or two.' He stepped forward.

Mel let him go in. He wished Niamh would stop looking at him like that. Mel would get suspicious.

They were both herded into the living room where Mel's husband was sitting, frowning at his phone. He looked up, took one look at Mel and said, 'I'll, er, just go check something in the other room,' and ran for it. Sensible man.

Tim wondered briefly how the retreat had gone in terms of mending relations between Mel and Alex.

'Sit,' Mel commanded.

Tim sat. Niamh flopped onto the sofa, her bottom lip tightening into a pout, suddenly all attitude. Mel stood over them, hands on her hips. 'Well,' she said, 'explain.'

'Nothing to explain, really,' said Tim. 'We thought it'd be nice to get away for a bit, so I took Niamh away, you know. Saw the sights. Hung out a bit. It was nice.' He tilted his head, stretching the side of his neck. 'I needed it, to be honest. Things at work were get — '

'Don't lie to me!' Mel paced in front of them. 'You always were a terrible liar, Tim.'

His mouth formed the words of protest but Mel stopped him. 'Don't even bother. I ask you one small thing and you screw it up. All the time you were lying to me about being in Reading, when all the while you were out there seeing . . . that woman.'

Niamh shot Tim a terrified glance. He knew how she felt. How the hell did Mel know?

'Your message made me suspicious,

so I checked where you were.' Mel turned to Niamh. 'You ... I'm disappointed in you, but I understand. You're just a child. That's why I left you with an adult.' She spun round to Tim. 'But you — '

'I'm not a child,' said Niamh.

'Yes you are.' Mel didn't even bother turning around.

Niamh sprang to her feet. 'Oh, so I don't count as a human being? I don't have feelings? And you wonder why I wanted to run away.'

Shit. Mel might have known where they were, but she couldn't have known about the running away. Oh, Niamh.

Mel turned slowly, eyes narrowed. 'What?'

Tim rose to his feet. 'She was going to run away. I found out. So we went up to Trewton together, okay? I didn't tell you because I didn't want to worry you.' He held out a hand in a placating gesture. 'She was perfectly safe. I was with her the whole time.'

Mel was still glaring at Niamh. 'You

tried to run away? To see your father's whore?' said Mel. 'Why would you want to do something so stupid?'

Ouch. That was the wrong thing to say, even he knew that.

'Because you don't understand. How could you? You never bloody listen to anything I say.' Niamh's hands were bunched into fists at her sides.

'I listen to you. I always listen to you. What the hell could you have to say to that bitch that you couldn't say to me?'

'Harriet is not a bitch.'

Tim groaned. Any goodwill that Niamh would have felt towards her mother after talking to Harriet was evaporating fast. He tried to intervene, but neither of them was paying him any attention.

'Don't you use that — '

'No. I'm not listening to you any-more.' Niamh stormed off, heading for the door.

'Where do you think you're going?' Mel snapped.

Niamh snapped back, 'I'm tired. I'm going to bed.'

Mel was practically glowing with rage. 'Get back here. I haven't finished with you.'

'Yes you have.' Niamh paused at the door. 'Harriet's much nicer than you ever were. No wonder Dad preferred her to you! I know I do!' With that, she clomped up the stairs.

Ouch. Even Tim was shocked at that. Mel, still staring at the doorway, seemed to shrink a little. Tim felt sorry for her. She must have been worried to cut short her holiday and return early. A blazing row was the last thing she needed right now.

'Mel,' he said gently, hoping she was all right.

Mel spun round, the anger back in her eyes. 'How dare she say that to me? After all the worry she's put me through. How — '

'Mel, stop,' said Tim. 'Try and understand what it's been like for Niamh — '

'Oh, it's all very well for you to say that. You're not off the hook yet, you know.' She pointed a finger at him. 'You lied to me. Went behind my back. Don't think I've forgotten.' Her eyes were narrowed, her features twisted into a scowl.

Tim stared at his sister and, for the first time, saw what other people had been trying to tell him for years. With Mel, it was all about her. He couldn't give enough to her. She would always demand more. Somehow he had fallen into this role of protector to his sister and never given it up. But right now the person who needed him wasn't his sister. It was his niece.

'I ask you to do one thing. I leave you with my precious little girl and you take her to see that bitch who ruined my marriage.'

Tim shook his head. 'Mel,' he said, louder than before, 'I said stop.'

He had never raised his voice to her before. It made her falter for a second before she stepped up to him, glaring. 'What?'

He didn't back down. Much as he loved his sister, he had to be here for

Niamh. 'This isn't about you, Mel. You need to stop going on the warpath or you're going to lose Niamh altogether.'

'Oh, you're telling me how to look after my child? Suddenly you're the childcare expert, are you? She ran away from you.'

'No, Mel. She ran away from you.' He saw her hesitate and pressed his advantage. 'She's desperately confused and unhappy. Her father died. She misses him. You won't let her talk about him. It's eating her up.'

Mel frowned. 'But it's been a year. I thought she'd be . . . ' She blinked. The frown deepened.

'You thought she'd be over it?' said Tim. 'I don't think it works like that. There isn't a time limit and then grief is over. It keeps coming. You just get better at dealing with it. Niamh's a teenager. Life is hard enough for her as it is and she's not dealing with it very well.'

The bluster went out of Mel. She turned and looked towards the door. 'But why didn't she tell me?'

'Would you have listened? You hate it when she talks about Richard. I know you took her to the funeral and did your best at the time, but how can Niamh talk to you when you grit your teeth every time someone mentions his name?'

'I don't.'

He raised his eyebrows at her.

She pressed her lips together. It was the closest she was going to get to an admission that he was right.

'Niamh needed to talk to someone about her dad. She loved him. And he loved her. So . . . she went to find the one person that she knew cared about him. She tried to run away, and when I found her, she was so distraught I thought it was best to let her talk to Harriet.' Okay, it wasn't exactly the truth, but it was close enough.

'You didn't have the right to do that. She's my daughter.'

'True,' he said. 'But if I had asked you, would you have let her go?'

'No. I don't want her anywhere near that whore.'

Tim winced. 'She's not a whore. Or a bitch. Or any of the things you call her. She's actually a nice, kind woman. And she did genuinely love Richard. I'm sorry, Mel. I know it wasn't what you wanted to hear, but — '

'I suppose she convinced you that she didn't steal Richard from me and Niamh.' Mel crossed her arms and raised her chin.

'No, actually, she didn't. She told Niamh that you were right and that Richard had been lying about when they got together.'

This seemed to confuse Mel completely. 'What? Why? I mean, why would she do that?'

'Like I said, she's a kind person. She saw that Niamh needed to build her bridges with you. Niamh needs you on her side right now, Mel. It would really, really help matters if you stopped shouting at her for ten minutes.'

Mel's lips pressed together so tightly that they almost disappeared.

Tim sighed. 'I know you don't want

to hear that, but it's true. Niamh is a great girl, Mel. Don't let her down.' He put his hands on her shoulders. She didn't push him off, which was a good sign.

'Listen,' he said. 'It's late. You need to talk to Niamh. I'm going to go home. Okay?'

She didn't answer. He took it as permission to leave.

'I'll call you tomorrow.' On an impulse, he leaned forward and kissed the top of her head. 'Goodnight, little sis.'

When he reached the door, he turned back to look at her. She had her arms crossed and was watching him, her expression unreadable. He gave her a tentative smile. She didn't smile back, but her expression softened a little. It was as good a result as any.

Once he was back in his car, Tim let out a long, shaky breath. Disagreeing with Mel was such an alien thing to do. He sent a message to Niamh. 'You okay?' He waited, but when there was no reply within a minute or so, he drove off. His flat was only about twenty-five minutes away. By the time he arrived, Niamh had written back.

'Yeah. Suppose. Thanks for what you said to Mum. Appreciate it. X'

Of course, she would have heard. He had been practically shouting. Tim smiled at the message. It was nice to be appreciated. He retrieved his bag from the back of the car and let himself in. His flat, in contrast to Mel's warm house, was dark and cold. He turned the heating up and kettle on. Standing, waiting for the kettle to boil, he took a deep breath. A wave of tiredness engulfed him. His back was stiff from the long drive, and now that he'd paused, he realised that his shoulders were solid knots of tension again. Arguing with Mel . . . he'd never really been much good at it. Already, guilt was niggling at him. He shouldn't have shouted at her. She was having a hard time. She needed him to support her, not to point out her failings. What kind of a brother was he?

He pulled out his phone and fired off a message to Mel.

'*Are you okay?*'

No reply. But then he hadn't expected one. The kettle clicked off. He made himself a tea, without milk, because there wasn't any. Tim sighed. Why did the women in his life have to be so difficult? Worse, why did they have to be at loggerheads with each other?

He wandered around his flat, throwing clothes in the wash, fishing out his shaving kit. He had a shower, put on clean pyjamas and felt the relief of being home. When he finally sank down to sit on the side of his bed, his limbs felt like they weighed a ton. He drank his tea and his thoughts drifted to Harriet, sitting in her own empty flat, with her ocean of sadness. He picked up his phone and sent her a message too. 'Back safe. Niamh delivered to her mother. Thanks for being so kind. Hope all is well with you.'

He wasn't expecting her to reply. He had turned in for the night before the realisation hit him. His eyes flew open. He had just thought of Harriet as a woman in his life. Oh dear. He'd hoped that once he was away from Trewton Royd he would forget about Harriet and his attraction to her would disappear, but what if it didn't? Just now he had thought of her with the same amount of affection and care that he had for Mel and Niamh.

It seemed that he liked Harriet more than he was willing to admit. He thought about that kiss the night before. Had it only been one day ago? It felt like ages. He checked his phone. No response from Harriet. He told himself it was probably for the best.

14

Harriet finished sending off more emails and shut down the laptop. It wasn't very late. She rubbed her face with her palms. It felt too quiet and lonely in here after having Niamh and Tim rattling around. It was just her now. No Richard to lift the monotony at the weekend. Just her. Living her little life above the shop. The sadness lapped at her, threatening to drag her back in. She needed company.

Crossing over to the window, she looked out at the lights of the pub. Company, if she wanted it, was never far away. All she had to do was cross the street. There was an unfinished conversation with Angie waiting for her there. It wasn't something she wanted to do, but it was necessary.

She had a sudden memory of Christmas, when the village had been snowed in. She had joined everyone else to make sure that the old and the frail were looked after. She had fallen in with the pulse of the village then. Been a genuine part of it. When people in the village needed her, she had been there for them. If she let them, perhaps they could be there for her too.

'There's only one way to find out.' Before she could change her mind, she grabbed her coat and bag and stamped out.

The pub was quiet, but not empty. It never was. Bill and Frank were propping up the bar, as usual. Angie was behind the bar. She gave Harriet a warm smile.

'Evening, love, what'll it be?' She took down a wine glass before she'd replied.

'Actually, I'd quite like a pint.' She wanted something she could nurse quietly for a while. If she had wine, it would go down too fast and she'd end up having another. She pointed out the lager she wanted.

Angie pulled the pint and passed it across. 'On the house.'

Harriet hoicked herself onto a bar stool at the other end of the bar to the two men. They both looked at her and she could see sympathy in their eyes.

'You all right, love?' said Frank. 'Now your visitors have gone.'

So it began. 'Yes, I'm okay. It's been an intense few days, but it was good to get things out in the open.'

The men exchanged glances. Angie leaned forward. 'We're very sorry to hear about your Richard. Why didn't you tell us? If we'd known . . . '

'What would you have done if you'd known, Angie? Pitied me? Tiptoed around me with sympathy?'

Sensing an uncomfortable conversation, one of the men at the bar said something loudly about the quiz machine and the two regulars shambled off.

Angie spared them a quick glance before turning her attention back to Harriet. 'No. We'd have been there for you. We'd have understood.'

226

'How could you understand, Angie?' Harriet looked down at her drink and felt her throat closing up at the thought of Richard's death. She thought she had finished crying. Apparently, there really was an ocean of tears inside her.

'You're not the first person to lose someone, Harriet. And you won't be the last.'

Angie's tone made her look up. The other woman was looking at her with a mixture of sympathy and steel. She realised suddenly that she knew very little about Angie's life outside of the village news. How had she not realised this before? In fact, what did she really know about any of the people in the village? Gossip, yes, but they all had pasts full of loves and losses that lay beneath the surface, just like she did. The tears continued to well up.

Angie came round the bar and gave her a hug. It was warm and comforting. The exact kind of human contact she needed. Harriet let herself be held. Not telling people, she realised, had been precisely the wrong thing to do. People weren't annoying. They were comforting.

After a few minutes, Harriet made an effort. She sniffed and drew away from Angie. 'Thank you.' She wiped her eyes. 'I needed that.'

'We all do, now and again,' said Angie. She leaned her elbows against the bar. 'Do you want to talk about it?'

Why the hell not. She had to do it at some point and it had been a year. Cautiously, she said, 'Richard was in a car accident.' She stopped. The world carried on existing. 'He was on his way here. To see me. It had been raining. He stopped at the traffic lights and . . . the lorry behind him didn't.'

Angie's face went through shock to sadness to sympathy in quick succession. 'Oh, Harriet,' she breathed. 'At least it was quick.'

That wasn't any consolation, but Harriet nodded.

'When was it?'

'About a year ago. Well, eleven

months and five days.'

'So long? You've been grieving by yourself all this time? Why didn't you tell us, love?'

Harriet took a sip of her pint, barely tasting it. 'If I told you, it would be true. So long as no one knew, I could pretend that it was just a normal week. That at the weekend, he'd show up.'

'But you can't keep on doing that, can you? That sort of thing makes people crack up.'

Harriet didn't say anything. She thought of the nights when she sat, huddled up into a bundle on the sofa, drinking glass after glass of wine, until the ache was replaced with the intense need to be held, to dance, to feel the hot press of a body against hers. Then there were the mornings where her head was shredded with pain and she hated herself. How she wondered how on earth she could explain to Richard why she'd kissed another man and how she remembered that Richard was no longer there to explain anything to.

That swift kick in the gut of grief that caught her afresh every time. Eventually, she would be sober enough to crawl back into denial and the whole thing would start again. *Yes, Angie. That sort of thing does make people crack up.*

The only time she behaved like a sane person was when she put on a 'normal' face in the shop or when she was out and about in the village. It was that veneer of normality that had saved her.

'I'm sorry,' she said.

'Nowt to be sorry about,' said Angie. 'Life doesn't come with instructions. We just muddle along as best we can.' She patted Harriet gently on the shoulder. 'You'll get there.'

There was a muttered argument going on by the quiz machine. One of the guys came up to the bar. Angie gave Harriet a last pat and hurried around to pull two more pints. 'You wouldn't know who won the Cricket World Cup in 1983, would you?' he asked Harriet.

Harriet shrugged.

Her phone buzzed. She opened the message. It was from Tim. A nice, friendly message. She smiled. A small flutter of interest in her chest. When she realised this, she stopped smiling. She put her phone away without replying to Tim's message. Life didn't come with instructions. Definitely not.

★　★　★

On Monday, Tim sat in his office and glared at his inbox. He had checked in with Niamh before he set off for work, and she'd said that Mel had insisted that they needed to spend quality time together and had booked them in to have their nails done that evening. Despite Niamh's tone, Tim could tell she was pleased. At least Mel had taken to heart what he'd said. She might not have forgiven him for saying it — she was still ignoring his calls — but at least she was doing something to mend bridges with Niamh.

It was strange being at odds with his

sister. They didn't often argue, mainly, he realised now, because he gave in to her all the time. To have her be angry with him was horrible. Normally, he would have picked up the phone and taken the first steps towards making peace, but this time . . . this time it was important that he didn't. He'd let Mel's childhood frailty and then Mel herself dictate their relationship for too long. No. He must hold firm.

He made an effort to focus on what he was doing. Emails. Emails. Ugh. So much dross. He marked the things he needed to do and stared at the list. He couldn't bring himself to do any of them. After a few minutes, his mind wandered over the miles back to Harriet. He seemed to spend a lot of time thinking about her. About the things she'd said, about the encompassing vastness of her grief, and late in the day, when his defences were weak, about the wine and coffee taste of her kiss.

He pulled up a paper he was drafting

and tried to write some more, but his mind was like sheet ice. Thoughts flailed around, unable to get purchase. Coffee. That was what he needed. A nice coffee. With one of those stupid patterns drawn in the foam. Yes, that was what he'd do. Grabbing his coat, he marched out of his office. It was the most decisive thing he'd done all day.

The route to the café took him past his former best friend Nick's office. Normally, he avoided looking at the all too familiar door, hurrying past it in case it opened. Today he paused. It had been a long time since he'd spoken to Nick. For the first time in ages, he was able to think about his friend without feeling like he was being wrung out. What had Harriet said? You can't choose how you fall in love. Nick had fallen in love with his best friend's girl and she had fallen right back. They had done the right thing. Okay, they could have waited a little longer, but who could blame them, really? They seemed, as far as he could tell from this distance, happy. What kind of a friend was he to begrudge them that?

This was one relationship that he could do something about. He didn't hate Nick. He missed him. If he wanted to rescue some of that friendship, one of them had to make the first move, and it might as well be him.

He knocked. There was a muffled 'come in'. Tim took a deep breath to prepare himself and stepped into his best friend's office.

Nick leaned back from his computer to see who it was and started. 'Tim.' He gathered himself and rose out of his chair.

'Hi,' said Tim. 'I was, er . . . ' He pointed to the corridor. 'I was going to grab a coffee and was wondering if you fancied one?'

Nick stared at him for a few seconds as though deciding how to deal with this, then said, 'Yeah. Sure. It's that time of day, right?' He picked up his jacket and walked around his desk. 'If you're sure you don't mind the company.'

'Not at all.' Tim smiled. He waited for Nick to lock his office door and they strode down the corridor together, neither of them speaking. This was going to be harder work than he'd thought.

They reached the door out of the building and stepped on to the pavement.

Nick said, 'Tim, about the whole me and Sarah thing. I . . . I'm sorry we hurt you.'

'It's okay. I'm sorry I was such an arse about it,' said Tim. 'It was just a bit . . . you know . . . '

They avoided looking at each other.

'Yes, I know,' said Nick. 'If it had been me, I'd probably have been the same, to be honest.'

There was a pause. A beat where things could go either way.

'No you wouldn't,' said Tim. 'You'd have been much worse. At least I'm only passive-aggressive.'

They looked at each other and both grinned. They carried on walking, but somehow Tim felt his step was lighter. Things were going to be okay with him and Nick.

15

It was a slow day in the shop. Harriet sat by the till and wondered what Niamh was doing. And Tim. What had he turned those amazing blue eyes towards now? She rested her chin on her hand and let her mind meander towards him. Would he ever come out from the shadow of his sister? Mel had so much power over him and he didn't even realise. She thought of him, sitting at her table, laughing and playing Monopoly. Of his face when he knelt to check on a sleeping Niamh. He clearly adored that girl. The only person who had more hold over Tim than Mel was Niamh . . . and she had no idea. Tim would face down anything for his niece. But would he face down his sister?

For a moment she allowed herself the fantasy of kissing Tim again. It set her stomach fluttering. The tendril of guilt that threaded through her feelings was diminished now. Richard was gone. She accepted it. With acceptance, she could relinquish the feeling that she belonged to Richard. She didn't belong to anyone. She knew that now. She had to move on.

Moving on required saying goodbye. Harriet had got a bag and collected Richard's things. There were a lot fewer than she'd imagined. A few items of clothing, mostly walking clothes, a pair of pyjamas, a couple of DVDs that she wouldn't ever watch by herself. All this she put in the bag. She decided to keep his favourite mug and the photos of him. Moving on didn't mean forgetting him entirely. Last of all, she took his razor and toothbrush out of the bathroom cabinet and put them in the bin.

It had taken her half an hour to drive out to the nearest charity shop collection bin. She stood in the damp car park and deposited everything in the chute. Once she got back, she felt a bit better, but it wasn't enough. Memories of Richard still trailed after her.

Harriet looked out of the window of the shop towards the hills. For so long now, she had been pretending that Richard wasn't gone, that he'd be turning up for the weekend. It was a difficult habit to break. There had to be some sort of closure. A line in the sand that said, 'I love you, I will always miss you, but I know you're not coming back.'

She needed to say goodbye. In order to do that, she had to go see him.

★   ★   ★

Tim paced around his kitchen, making himself dinner and checking his phone every few minutes. Still nothing from Mel. Five days now. Niamh was fine, but Mel was not speaking to him. Five. Days. He picked up the phone, just as he had done several times that evening, then put it back down again. No. He had to stand firm. It was always him that phoned. Always. If he allowed himself to cave in and call her, nothing would change. Except he hated this. He felt like he was letting everyone down, like everything was his fault.

He sighed, got himself a bowl of chilli and stood over the phone, watching it. *What is this hold she has over you?* Harriet had asked. Tim ladled a forkful of food into his mouth. Perhaps that was the question he should have asked himself. Perhaps he should have asked not why Mel demanded so much of him . . . but why he kept giving in.

This was the role assigned to him. The protective twin. She was the sickly twin. He was the strong one. Somewhere along the line, the dynamic had blurred. He needed her to need him.

Slowly, he lowered his fork. She wasn't the needy one. He was. For all his complaining that Mel and Niamh came to him for support, he needed that. Being the supportive man had become part of his definition of himself. Even Harriet, he realised. He had only let her in when he'd seen her distress and stepped in to be her support. Except it hadn't been him she'd needed. It was Niamh. All he had done was make tea and annoy her. When he had pulled away from kissing her, she'd thrown him out.

The thought made him smile. He needed to get over himself. If there was any woman in his life who didn't need him, it was Harriet. She seemed to be managing life just fine. Grieving, yes, but still coping. She was stronger than anyone he'd met before.

Tim had a vivid memory of her, arms wrapped around herself, as though holding herself together, chin raised. 'I'm not anyone's. I'm mine.' Lovely, determined Harriet, who listened to him and listened to Niamh; who told Niamh an unpleasant truth because she didn't want Niamh to lose touch with her mother. Harriet, who had lost touch with her own family.

He finished his meal, still standing over the phone, which still did not ring.

Thoughts of Harriet circled round his mind. How was she? Did she think about him, like he was thinking about her? He missed her. A strong, insistent tug. He had not intended to keep in touch with her. Mel would not approve, but . . .

Oh stuff it. Mel didn't run his life. If he wanted to talk to Harriet, he would. He picked up the phone and called her number. It rang. He had a flash of panic. What was he going to say? He nearly hung up, but she answered before he could.

'Hello?'

Her voice had the strangest effect on him. Blood deserted his brain for a second. He wanted nothing more than to jump in the car and drive straight back to Trewton Royd to see her.

'Hello? Who is this?'

'Oh. Hi. It's me. Er . . . Tim.'

There was a pause, as though she were trying to figure out how to respond to him. Finally, she said, 'Hi, Tim. What can I do for you?'

What did he want? He'd called just to make contact. To hear her voice. 'I, um, just wanted to see how you were,' he said.

'That's kind of you, Tim. I'm okay, thanks. You?'

'Oh. I'm fine. Um . . . ' God, this was embarrassing. What on earth was he doing?

'How's Niamh?' asked Harriet.

'Not bad. Her mother found out where we'd been.'

There was a little gasp down the line. 'Oh no. What happened?'

He had meant to give a summary, but it all came pouring out. When he got to the part where he'd argued with Mel, Harriet said, 'Have you caved in and called her yet?'

'No. I wasn't going to.'

She laughed. A warm, sexy sound. 'You so were.'

'I wasn't.' He realised he was smiling. 'Anyway, enough about me. What have you been up to.'

She was quiet for a few seconds. 'I

cleared out Richard's stuff. Took it . . . took it to the charity shop. He's not going to use it now.'

Another pause.

'Are you okay?' Tim asked. Clearing out Richard's things must have been hard for her.

'Yes,' she said. 'I think it helped. But I also think that I should see him. The grave, I mean. And say goodbye.'

Tim's heart shouldn't have thumped the way it did. 'That's a good idea. If you need a place to stay while you're here . . . I have a spare room.' Aaaaah. Why did he just say that? He would have to tidy the place up. He looked around at the piles of paper and books. His gaze strayed towards his room. How could he cope with her being in the same place? He couldn't take it back now. Hopefully she wouldn't want to stay at his.

'Actually, if you didn't mind, I might take you up on that,' she said quietly.

Oh crap. 'Are you sure? I completely understand if you'd rather not stay in the flat of a strange man.'

'You're not that strange,' she said, the laughter back in her voice. 'But I completely understand if you've just changed your mind about opening up your abode to a strange woman.'

It was the hint of laughter that did it. She was teasing him. He hadn't had that level of ease with someone, apart from Nick, in years. He laughed. 'You are pretty strange, but I'll cope, I think.'

'Cheeky bugger.'

They arranged dates and times. She promised to email him the times for her train. By the time he hung up, he was smiling broadly, the tension from earlier in the evening forgotten.

* * *

He was settling down to do some work when the doorbell rang. Tim frowned. He wasn't expecting anyone. He never had unexpected visitors. The bell rang again. Still frowning, he opened the door.

'Mel. What's . . . ' He was going to ask her what was wrong, almost by reflex. He reminded himself that he wasn't her fixer. 'Hi.'

'Are you just going to stand there scowling? Or are you going to invite me in?' she said.

'Sure, but I'm a bit busy.' He moved aside. 'So it'll have to be a short visit.'

She stood in the middle of the living room and looked at the table where his work lay spread out. 'Working?'

'Yes. I do have to.' He put his hands on the back of the chair he had been sitting on. 'What can I do for you, Mel?'

'I'm not sure.' She frowned. Blinked. Then pulled out a chair and sat down.

Tim resisted the urge to roll his eyes. 'Well, you came all the way over, so you might have some idea.'

'I . . . spent the afternoon with Niamh today,' said Mel. She hadn't taken her coat off, but fiddled with the cuffs.

Tim moved his own chair and sat down. 'And?'

'And it was nice. You . . . you were

right.' She looked up. There was a faint air of puzzlement about her. 'She's much nicer when we're relaxed in each other's company.'

'That's not what I said.'

'No, but it amounts to the same thing,' said Mel.

He let that pass.

'Anyway, she told me some things. She said she spent some time with Harriet and that it really helped.' Mel frowned. 'She made Harriet out to be some sort of saint and I'm pretty sure she isn't. I mean, what sort of saint steals another woman's husband?'

It took effort not to respond and tell her that Harriet hadn't known. That Richard had lied to them both. He knew if he said that, Mel would go off on a tangent. He waited.

'But,' said Mel, after a few seconds, 'it was good that Harriet finally told her the truth. Niamh even apologised for not believing me.' Mel looked up. 'Can you believe that? Niamh. Apologising. She never apologises for anything.'

'Yeah. Wonder who she gets that from.' He smiled at her.

She narrowed her eyes at him. 'If you're expecting me to apologise for shouting at you, you're going to have a long wait.'

He shook his head. 'No. I understand why you were angry. I lied to you about where she was. But she was safe the whole time. I really think she needed to talk to someone who loved her father as much as she does.'

'Did he really? Love Harriet, I mean.'

'I think he probably did. She certainly loved him.'

'What does she have that I don't?'

What? How was he supposed to answer that? Trust Mel to think of this as some sort of competition. 'I don't think it works like that, Mel. You're totally different to each other. I think by the time he met her, you and he had already fallen out of love with each other. It's not that he chose her over you.' He leaned forward and patted her hand. 'People change. The young guy that fell in love with you was different to the older guy who left you. It's not Harriet's fault. Or Niamh's. Or even yours. It just happened.'

To his utter horror, Mel's eyes filled with tears. 'I don't want that to happen with me and Niamh.'

'Oh, Mel.' He had no defence against his sister's tears. All at once he was back in the hospital room, where his immunocompromised sister stretched out a hand and begged him to take her out to play. At the time he had been fully togged up in mask, gown, over-shoes and gloves so that he didn't pass on anything infectious to her. All he could do was cover her hand with his own, with the plastic of his gloves in between them and give her a gentle squeeze. He hadn't been able to help her then. He couldn't refuse to help her ever again. He went over and put his arms around her. 'You'll just have to work at it to make sure it doesn't happen.'

He let her weep on him for a few minutes. When she was calmer, he asked, 'How did it go on the retreat? Are things okay with you and Alex?'

Mel fished around in her handbag and found her tissues. 'I think so. He said some things. I said some things . . . but in the end, I think it's okay.' She blew her nose. 'Am I demanding and controlling, Tim? Really?'

'He said that?' Brave man.

'But is it true?'

He considered the easy option. No. That was what had trapped him in the first place. If he was going to change the dynamic of their relationship, he had to be honest, even if he knew she wouldn't like it. 'Sometimes,' he said. 'You have a tendency to look at things only from your perspective. Not everyone sees things the same way.'

When she didn't bite his head off, he continued, 'Sometimes, you have to accept that people have to do what they need to do. Even if you think they're being stupid.'

She gave it some thought. 'Like you deciding to take a job in academia, you mean?' she said. 'Just because you didn't want to go out into the real world and get a real job.'

'It is a real job.' He shook his head. Some arguments he was never going to win. 'Look, since you're here, would you like a cup of tea?'

'I thought you said you were busy.' She indicated the pages lined up on the desk.

'I am. But I always have time for my little sister.' As he said it, he realised it was true. He could fight it all he liked, but if Mel ever genuinely needed him, he would be there for her. Because he loved her. The knowledge settled inside him. Now he knew. He would work around it.

Mel looked at him, her expression thoughtful, for what seemed like ages. 'You're a good brother,' she said at last.

He smiled. 'I try to be.'

'I realise ... ' She paused and seemed to have a moment of indecision before plunging on. 'I realise that I'm not always the most understanding person and I haven't always been . . . there for you like you have been for me.' She swallowed. 'But I do love you, you know.' Her eyes met his. 'I'm just not very good at showing it.'

Until she'd said it, he hadn't realised how much he'd needed to hear it. All those years of watching out for her, worrying on her behalf. All of it was done out of love. It was nice to know that it was appreciated. 'I know,' he said. 'But if you could try to be a bit more understanding . . . '

Mel nodded. 'That's what Niamh said. I'll try. You'll have to remind me from time to time.'

'I'm sure I can do that.' Tim grinned.

Mel blew her nose delicately. 'I should be going.' She stood up. 'I told Alex I wouldn't be long. I told him not to let Niamh out of the house, and the atmosphere at home is a little strained.'

No wonder. He drew a breath to remind her that she was meant to be repairing relations with Niamh, but she cut him off.

'I know. I know. But she ran away. I can't let that go without comment.' She hitched up her handbag. 'The next time she says she needs to talk about something, can you let me know? I don't want her running off to that Harriet woman again. She says she's keeping in touch and I can't stop that, but I don't intend to let her go off and visit.'

Uh oh. He had just arranged for Harriet to come and visit him and, by extension, Niamh. Should he mention it? He didn't want to upset the fragile peace between Mel and Niamh or between Mel and himself.

While he was paralysed by indecision, Mel had reached the door. 'I'll see you later, Tim,' she said, all business once more. 'Thanks for the chat.'

'Any time,' he said. Harriet wasn't due to come visit for a couple of weeks. No need to worry Mel by mentioning it just yet.

16

Harriet strode towards the station entrance and searched for Tim's lanky frame in the people who were waiting. Nothing. She had a flare of panic. If he didn't show up, she would have nowhere to stay overnight. The train ticket had cost her almost everything her overdraft would allow. She had a small cash budget and that was it. It probably wasn't enough to pay for a room in a Premier Inn. She hitched her bag up on her shoulder. Oh well. If she needed to sleep in the station concourse, she would. All she needed to do was visit Richard's grave and get back home.

She pulled out her phone to check for messages. There was one.

Will be 10 mins late. Tim.

Okay, so he was coming. Should she part with a bit of precious cash and get herself a coffee? She ambled over to the shop. A couple of buckets of flowers caught her eye. Tim was taking her to Richard's grave. She stared at the meagre selection of bouquets. Flowers were the right thing to take to a grave, but Richard would have preferred a newspaper. Or a book of crossword puzzles. The sudden image sprang up of Richard lying on the sofa frowning over the crossword. The memory brought with it a wave of sadness. Her breath caught. She let it fall over her, submerge her . . . and then it passed. She looked down at the flowers again. No, not flowers. She picked up a copy of a newspaper. She paid for a carrier bag as well.

Thoughts of Richard still caught her out at the strangest moments, but she was getting better at dealing with them now. They no longer brought her to her knees. Somehow, that weekend with Niamh and Tim had punctured the balloon of hurt in her chest and shrunk it down to something that allowed her to carry on breathing.

As she left the shop, she spotted Tim. A small bubble of happiness rose in her. He looked less tired than he had done when she last saw him. Apart from that, he looked exactly the same. This pleased her more than she'd imagined.

He saw her a second later and they moved towards each other. What did she do when they met in the middle? Did she shake his hand? Hug him? Kiss him on the cheek? How did you greet a man that you fancied, but was also a friend?

He solved the problem by saying, 'I'm really sorry, but we'll have to hurry. I've parked illegally and the wardens are prowling around.' He headed off back to the exit almost before he'd finished speaking. Gratefully, she hurried after him.

In the car, he asked her if she wanted to drop her bag off and have a cup of tea first, or head straight to the graveyard.

'Straight there, please,' she said. 'I bought him this.' Immediately, she realised she shouldn't have said anything.

'A newspaper?'

'For the crossword.' Which wasn't much of an explanation. 'He liked to do the crossword.'

If Tim thought this explanation sounded mad, he didn't show it. He nodded. '*Guardian* or *Times*?'

'*Times*.'

Tim nodded again. 'I'm a *Guardian* man, myself.'

They lapsed into silence for a bit. Harriet entertained herself by looking out of the window and occasionally sneaking glances at Tim's long legs. She liked good legs on a man. She remembered Tim sitting at her table in a T-shirt that was too small for him. If his lean arms were anything to go by, he would have good legs. Hot on the heels of these thoughts came a hint of guilt. What would Richard say?

She gripped the newspaper, carefully wrapped in the plastic bag. The last time she'd been here was for the funeral.

Her memories of that awful day were a blurred mess of sorrow, awkwardness and hostility. She wondered how she'd cope with being back there, where Richard's body had been interred next to his grandparents, in the town where he'd spent most of his life. He had been hers for such a short time.

The cemetery was not far out of town. Tim parked up and turned towards her. 'Ready?'

The concern on his face melted her. Tim was a good man. She wondered how she could ever have thought him irrelevant. She nodded and let herself out of the car. Weak sun shone on the tidy cemetery. She didn't know where she needed to go. Somehow, she'd thought she'd remember. A quick search in her bag and she brought out the print out of the directions she'd got off the cemetery website.

Tim cleared his throat. 'Do you want me to come with you?' he said, not meeting her eyes.

It was an awkward situation. Richard

had once been Tim's brother-in-law. She knew he wouldn't have any desire to visit Richard's grave . . . but now that she was here, she suddenly didn't want to go on alone. 'Please,' she said. 'If . . . if you don't mind.'

Blue eyes flashed up at her. 'Of course.'

They walked in silence, Harriet checking her map from time to time. She felt the curious push-pull of emotion. As much as she wanted to move on, part of her wanted to keep things exactly as they were. Things weren't so bad, were they?

Richard's grave was small and plain, which was exactly what he'd have wanted. His family, elderly parents and two brothers, had dealt with the funeral. Harriet, as the mistress, had been reluctantly informed. No one had spoken to her. The grave wasn't overgrown, but not as neat as some of the others. Someone was looking after it.

Tim said, 'I'll just be over there if you need me,' and withdrew, leaving her standing in front of the grave. Just her and the mortal remains of Richard. Essentially, she was alone.

Harriet placed her little parcel down where the flowers should go. 'I brought you the crossword,' she said. There was nothing but the sound of leaves rustling, the distant hum of traffic and the coo of a woodpigeon somewhere nearby. It was as though the world was listening, waiting for her to speak.

'Thank you for sending Niamh to see me.' She had given up being rational about it. This was the best explanation that she could come up with. Richard was gone, but he'd sent her and Niamh to each other, so that they could support each other in his absence.

'I gave your stuff to charity,' she confessed. 'I'm sorry. I know . . . I know it means losing my connection with you, but I can't carry this pain any longer. I'm so sorry, Richard.' Tears she'd not even noticed welling up, trickling down to her chin. 'I don't want to forget you. Neither does Niamh. But we both need to get on with being alive.'

She pulled out a tissue and wiped the tears away. The tranquillity of the place surrounded her. She had the strangest feeling that Richard had acknowledged what she'd said, and that he didn't mind. He was watching out for her. He wanted her to move on.

She glanced around, half expecting to see him. The only other person there was Tim, standing hunched and ill at ease, not far away. Turning back to the gravestone, she whispered, 'Did you send him to me?'

There was burst of noise and a bird took off, making her jump as it flew past her head. As she fought her breath back under control, a feather floated down in front of her. She caught it in her palm. It was white.

Her mother had always told her that white feathers were fallen from angels. Harriet herself didn't believe in heaven and hell, but people must go somewhere. She stared at the feather in her hand and wondered where her baby went when she died, before she'd even had a chance to see the world. She pressed the fingers of her other hand to her chest, where she felt the emptiness. 'Look after my baby, Richard,' she whispered.

As she dropped her hand, she felt a lightness in her shoulders. She had said goodbye not to one person, but two. And they were together now, pulled to each other by their connection to her. Somehow it made all the difference to know that.

Harriet said, 'Thank you.'

She carefully stowed the feather in her coat pocket and glanced across at Tim. It was time to stop feeling guilty about how she felt. Then she blew her nose, squared her shoulders and set off to take on the future.

* * *

Tim shoved his hands in his pockets and wished he'd stayed in the car. He wasn't sure why he'd accompanied Harriet here. It wasn't like she couldn't find her way herself. Yet he couldn't bear to let her go alone, weighed down as she was by her grief. So he loitered at a crossroads, resisting the urge to pull out his phone.

He watched Harriet bow her head. She was different to anyone he'd met before. Less career driven, more independent in her own way. Was that what attracted him to her? He had given up denying to himself that he fancied her. He did. That kiss — the one he'd completely ruined — could have been a rebound thing, but the way he kept thinking about her, and the way his heart had kicked up a notch when he saw her at the station . . . those things told him it wasn't a temporary thing. Now, he'd stupidly invited her to come and stay.

She was still grieving. It was obvious. There was no way she would want anything more than friendship. But there was that kiss.

He reflected on what she'd said about being lonely. *Sometimes, when I have a drink, I get so . . . desolate. I need someone to hold me.* That was all he had been to her. Someone to hold her and keep the desolation away. A desire founded by alcohol and her missing Richard. Nothing special. He should remember that. He looked back at her. He would keep his cool. It was just a crush. You could fancy someone and be in the same room as them without making an idiot of yourself. It was called being an adult.

That was what he would do. Be a friend. That was all. And once Harriet left, that would be it. He need never see her again. He looked towards where she was standing. Why did that thought make him feel so awful?

As he watched, she touched her chest and was still for a moment. When she looked up, he could almost see her pull herself together. She drew back her shoulders and straightened her spine. She turned and walked towards him. As she got closer, he could see the redness in her eyes and the smudge of mascara where she'd wiped away tears — those vulnerabilities that she had pushed down out of sight. The sun caught her hair and made it glow red. She smiled at him. His heart thundered in response. And he knew that he was in trouble. This was no passing infatuation. He was in love.

17

Harriet had felt progressively lighter with every passing minute since leaving the graveyard. It was as though the cloud of grey that she'd worn around herself was finally peeling off, letting the real Harriet emerge. Some of this, she had to admit, was because of Tim. The more time she spent with him, the more she liked him. More than liked him. If she felt this strongly about him when she was sober, she'd best be careful not to drink too much around him.

She and Tim were sitting in his flat, eating Chinese food using chopsticks. It had started off as a joke, but neither of them had been willing to give up. It was silly, but it lent the meal a sense of fun and camaraderie that made it easier for them to talk. And talk they did. So far they had covered a range of topics from village news to work to world politics. Right now, Tim was telling her about how Mel had apologised to him for the first time ever.

'I'm glad,' she said. 'If you didn't ever call out her behaviour, she'd just carry on thinking it was acceptable.'

Tim nodded. The prawn on his chopsticks dropped back into his bowl. He picked it out again. 'You're very wise, you know,' he said. 'Especially what you said about Niamh. She and Mel are getting on much better now.'

'Good.' She meant it. Niamh was a lovely girl. She deserved to be understood better. 'It's really good that she's getting on with her mum again. It's an awful thing to not be able to talk to your mother.' She hadn't spoken to her own parents in fifteen years. She'd picked up the phone many a time, but never plucked up enough courage to make the call.

She looked up from her bowl to find Tim watching her. 'What?'

'Do you talk to your mother, ever?'

For a second she was startled, until she remembered that she'd told him about it on the night that he'd kissed her. There were very few people who knew about her life before. She shook her head.

'Have you tried to get in touch?'

She looked down at her food and shook her head again. 'My dad's pretty stubborn,' she murmured. 'My mum pretty much goes along with what he says.'

There was a soft plink as he put his bowl down. 'How do you know that things haven't changed?' he said. 'They may miss you too.'

She raised her gaze to his. 'How do you know I miss them?'

His eyebrows rose a fraction, one rising higher than the other. 'Don't you?'

He had her there. 'Yes,' she said.

'Then call them,' he said. 'Or write. Keep trying.'

The one letter she'd sent had been returned unopened. Her parents didn't even know about the baby. She pulled a face. 'My dad was a pillar of the community. I embarrassed him. He won't talk to me.'

'If you don't try to change the situation, it'll just carry on looking acceptable,' he said. He gave her a tiny, half hesitant smile. God, that was sexy.

She smiled back. 'Fine. I'll try again.'

'Good.' He picked up the bottle of wine that was on the table and topped up both their glasses.

'Woah. I hope you're not trying to get me drunk.' She said it to lighten the mood, but the minute the words came out, she saw him tense.

'I'm sorry,' he said. 'I should have asked.' The relaxed atmosphere between them frosted over.

'I was joking.'

'But you're right. I should have checked.' He wouldn't meet her eyes now. What was going on?

After a few minutes, he said, 'I don't know about you, but I'm stuffed. I couldn't eat another thing.'

'Uh, yeah. Me too.' It was mostly true. She stood up. 'Let me help you.'

They put lids on the leftovers, working methodically, but no longer chatting.

Harriet watched Tim as he knelt in front of the small fridge, trying to stack the boxes in between whatever else he usually kept in there. What had just happened? One minute they were talking easily, the next minute this awkwardness.

She leaned against the work surface. 'Tim?'

'Hmm?' He found a space for the last container. 'Gotcha. There.' He stood up, closing the fridge door as he did so. He didn't turn to look at her.

'Is something wrong?'

The stiffening of his shoulders were a bit of a giveaway. 'No.' He turned slowly. 'Why do you ask?'

'Because you've been acting weird ever since I made that crack about the wine.'

He didn't reply for a moment, just looked at her, with a tiny frown line between his eyes. She studied his face and couldn't understand what she saw there.

'Was it something I said?' she asked.

He sighed. 'It's not you. It's me. I remembered what you said about the desolation when you've had too much to drink. And this . . . friendship.' He gestured between them. 'I don't want you to think that I would try to push it further.'

Oh bugger. She'd hoped to do just that. 'Why not? Does your sister object to you having contact with me?'

'No. I mean, yes, she does, but that's not it.'

She took a step closer to him. 'Then what?' Get on with it. Spit it out. Up close, he was handsome. You saw past the cute smile and the nice forearms and saw the kindness, the genuine desire to help. A good man. She remembered what it was like to kiss him. A very good man.

'I like you, Harriet. I really, really like you.' He finally met her gaze and she saw the want in it. Heat flared inside her. She stepped closer. Almost by reflex, his hands came up and rested on her hips.

'And?' she said. 'I like you too. This doesn't sound very complicated.'

'But you're in a strange place right now.'

She stilled. 'Are you going to tell me I'm Richard's again?' Surely he knew her better than that.

'No, not at all. You're not anybody's. That's the problem. I really want you to be . . . mine.'

They were so close now, she could feel his chest move when he breathed. Her breath mingled with his. She understood that doubt in his eyes. He wanted her to be sure that she wasn't just sleepwalking into a new relationship. He wanted her, but he needed her to be sure she wanted him. It was that hesitation that undid her. A level of consideration that she hadn't even realised she'd needed until he'd offered it to her.

'I'm not ready to be yours,' she said,

softly. She put a finger to his lips and traced the line of his mouth. His fingers tightened on her hips. He closed his eyes and his breath was warm against her fingertip.

'How about,' she said. 'I agree to be . . . ours.'

His eyes flew open. He smiled, a slow, wicked smile that set her on fire. She moved her finger onto his lip again. He took it in his mouth and she felt every single synapse from her fingertip to her groin.

He slid his hands around her, so that she was pulled even tighter against him. 'Works for me,' he said and kissed her. It was every bit as wonderful as she'd imagined. She felt the need inside opening up, wanting more. She reached down and pulled at his shirt. This time, he didn't stop her.

★   ★   ★

A few weeks after Harriet's visit, Tim went to see Mel and Niamh. He wasn't entirely sure what reception he'd get when he rang the bell. He'd exchanged a few messages with Mel, but not really spoken to her at any great length. Part of the reason for this was because he didn't trust himself not to let slip about himself and Harriet.

What with one thing and another, he hadn't even told Niamh that Harriet had been in town.

Mel opened the door, the telephone tucked against one ear, and waved him inside. She gave him a smile, pointed to the phone, and rushed off to the study. Left alone in the hallway, Tim popped his head into the lounge. Alex was sitting in front of the telly with the *Financial Times* open on his lap. Tim couldn't tell which one he was paying more attention to.

'Evening, Alex,' Tim said.

Alex waved but didn't look up. Tim withdrew his head and made for the kitchen. There was coffee in the machine, so he poured himself a mug. Niamh would be up in her room. He pulled out his phone and called her.

'Hi, Uncle Tim. How're you?'

'I'm downstairs in your kitchen, if you wanted to ask me face to face,' he said.

'Oh cool. Be down in a minute.'

A few minutes later there was the thunder of a teenager running down the stairs, and Niamh appeared. 'I haven't seen you in ages,' she said by way of a greeting. She fetched herself some orange juice from the fridge.

'How've you been?' Tim dropped his voice. 'How are things going with your mum?'

Niamh slid into the chair next to his. 'They're okay,' she said. 'For a while Mum did all this 'mother and daughter bonding' stuff, but she's laid off that now.'

Tim frowned. 'Does that mean things are going back to the way they were before?'

Niamh made a so-so motion with her hand. 'Not exactly,' she said. 'But close.' She shrugged. 'At least she found me a box of photos from her life with Dad.

They're like, really young in them.'

'Good. I'm glad things are improving,' said Tim.

Niamh gave a one-shouldered shrug, which Tim took to mean that she agreed. Or at least didn't disagree.

He took a careful sip of coffee. Now would be a good time to tell Niamh about Harriet, especially as Mel wasn't around. 'Have you been in touch with Harriet at all?' he said. He knew she had been, because Harriet had told him so.

'Yeah. She's cool. I photographed some of the photos of Dad for her — the ones without Mum in.'

He nodded. 'She said.'

'Have you been in touch with her, then?' said Niamh.

Tim felt his ears going red.

'Uncle Tim?' Niamh leaned forward and stared at him. She gave a sudden squeal. 'You and Harriet?' She clapped her hands and hooted with laughter. 'That's brilliant!'

'You're okay with it?' Relief washed

through him. At least Niamh was going to be on his side.

'Of course I am. Why wouldn't I be?'

'I dunno. I thought maybe you'd be upset that she'd been here and hadn't seen you.'

'Wait. She was here? When? How long for? How come you never said?'

This was the bit he was worried about. 'She came to say goodbye to your dad. She wasn't here for very long, just one night and . . . I, well, we didn't think it was a good idea to annoy your mum so close to things.'

'You could have made up something. You didn't have to tell Mum!' Niamh said, her voice climbing to volume.

The door to the kitchen opened and Mel came in. 'Tell me what?'

Niamh shot Tim a look, but he knew he already looked guilty as hell. Mel's eyes narrowed. 'Tell me what? Tim?'

Tim sighed. He may as well do this now. There was no point dragging it out for more weeks. 'That I'm seeing Harriet.'

'What? When? What does she want?'
Mel put her hands on her hips.

Niamh gave a snort. 'No, Mum. He's
seeing Harriet. You know, like going out
with her.'

Mel turned to look at Tim. Her face
went pale. Her mouth made shapes but
no words came out.

'It's a long-distance thing,' he said.
'We're taking things slowly.' He watched
Mel carefully. Her lips compressed. She
was about to go nuclear.

'First Richard and now you?' Mel
shouted. 'What does that woman have
against me?'

Even though he had been expecting
something like this, he was still shocked.
'It's not about you, Mel,' he said. 'It's
about me and Harriet. And how we feel
about each other.'

'How could you?'

'Mum! Seriously?' said Niamh.

'You, go to your room. This isn't a
conversation that concerns you,' Mel
snapped.

'Actually, it does,' Niamh shouted

back. 'Harriet's my friend.'

Mel drew a breath. Tim stood up. 'Enough.' He put a hand up to stop Niamh's next comment.

'Ti — ' Mel began.

'I said, enough. Mel, just listen for one second. I understand this is weird for you. It's weird for me too. But I really like Harriet. So stop for one moment, okay? Give me a chance to see how this works out.'

When she opened her mouth to speak again, he did something he'd never done before. He asked for her help. 'Please,' he said. 'I need you to do this. For me.'

In the silence that followed, Niamh stood up and moved to stand beside him. He gave her a grateful glance. She punched him gently on the shoulder.

Mel's gaze moved from one to the other. When neither of them moved, her anger seemed to deflate. Slowly, her shoulders dropped. 'You're sure about this?'

Tim said, 'Yes.'

Niamh added, 'I think we should let

them find out if it's going to work out.'

Mel nodded and looked away. 'Okay.' She raised her eyes back to Tim. 'Are you planning to move up to Yorkshire?'

'Not at the moment,' he said. 'But if things work out, maybe. I don't know yet.'

Mel pulled out a chair and sat down. 'Right.'

Tim and Niamh exchanged a glance. This was good. Slowly, Tim sat back down.

'If this all goes horribly wrong,' Mel said, pointing a finger at Tim, 'don't come to me for sympathy.'

Tim smiled. 'I won't.'

'Okay.'

'Okay.'

There was a tense silence. Finally, Niamh moved across to her mother and gave her a hug. Mel looked surprised.

'I know how hard this is for you Mum,' said Niamh. 'I'm proud of you.' She grinned at Tim. 'And you, Uncle Tim. Harriet's awesome. She'd make a cool aunty.'

Both Tim and Mel protested and Niamh laughed. 'You guys are so serious,' she said. 'I'm going to go call Harriet. I can't believe you've kept it quiet for so long.' She ran off upstairs.

Brother and sister sat in the kitchen in silence. Finally, Tim said, 'Mel . . . thank you. It means a lot that you're not trying to . . . ' He stopped. He wasn't sure what word he was looking for. 'Sabotage' was too strong. 'I know you're not pleased, but I appreciate you're being calm about it.'

Mel gave him a small smile. 'It's okay,' she said. 'The other day you said you'd always be there for me.'

'Yes.'

'Well maybe it won't kill me to return the favour sometimes.'

Tim reached a hand across the table. Mel took it and squeezed.

18

Harriet ran up the stairs after shutting up the shop. It was still light outside and the sun slanted in through the window. She shut the door and admired the new throw she'd bought from the craft shop in the village — a colourful crochet affair which brightened up the flat no end. She had another half an hour before Tim was due to arrive and she still hadn't made the call she'd promised she'd make. He wouldn't mind, of course, but the only reason she'd told him was so that she would force herself to do it.

She sighed and went over to the phone. No point putting it off. She took a deep breath and, still standing, dialled the number she knew by heart. The ringing tone kicked in. She imagined the phone trilling in her parents' over-warm living room. It sat on a low table next to her mother's chair. At least it had, the last time she'd seen it. That had been fifteen years ago. She had been a different person then.

There was a click. 'Hello.'

It was her father. She had been expecting her mother to pick up and hearing her father's deep voice stalled her.

'Hello? Hello?' he said. 'This better not be another bloody auto call thing.'

'Dad.'

Silence. It stretched, a tangible, solid thing.

'Dad, it's me. Harriet. How . . . how are you?'

There was a small noise on the other end, part gasp, part grunt. Then he said, 'I told you never to call here again.' And the line went dead.

Harriet stood for a moment, holding the phone to her ear, even though he was gone again. What had she expected? She had changed, but her parents didn't know that. She sighed and put the phone back in its cradle. At least she'd tried.

Feeling heavy and sad, she set out the tins of soup and the fresh bread rolls from the bakery, ready for when Tim arrived. She smiled at the thought. He came up most weekends now. He'd started joking that Trewton Royd was his weekend holiday home. He tended to bring work with him, but she didn't really mind. She was getting a trickle of copywriting clients back and it was nice to sit next to each other on the sofa, working. It was an altogether more relaxed relationship than she'd had with Richard. Tim gave her companionship and support that she hadn't even realised she'd needed. Yes, she had changed. It had taken her a long time to realise it.

She checked the wall clock and decided that she had time to go have a shower before Tim got there. As she was heading into her room, the phone rang. She answered it, expecting it to be Tim.

'Hello?' said a quiet voice. 'Harriet?'

The voice was frailer, more timorous,

284

but oh, so familiar. 'Mum?' Her throat felt tight. 'Mum, is that you?'

'Oh,' said her mother. 'Oh good. I was hoping that if I did 1471, I would get you. I'm so sorry your dad . . . well. He doesn't know I'm calling you. He's gone out to talk to Walter next door and I thought . . . oh, it's good to hear from you, love. How are you?'

'I'm okay, Mum. I really am. How are you?'

'Well, not as healthy as I was, you know, but not too bad.' There was a pause as they both tried to work out what to say next. 'How is your . . . young man?'

It had been so long. Her mother knew nothing about her separation from her first partner, or Richard . . . or the baby. 'Oh Mum, that didn't work out. We split up years ago. Years and years. I tried to call you at the time, but . . . '

'Oh, I know, love. Your father's a proud man. I think he really regrets how he reacted, but well, you know what he's like. He can't admit a mistake.'

The tone of her voice made Harriet smile. It reminded her of those rare moments when she and her mother had shared an understanding. 'I know,' she said.

'Listen, love, your father's coming back. I have to go. Can I call you? From time to time?'

'Of course you can!' Relief, cool and sweet, flooded through her. Her mother wanted to keep in touch. 'Even better, Mum. I can come and see you one day. Meet in town, for a tea, maybe?'

'I'd like that.' She was speaking quickly now. 'You take care, love. Bye.'

Harriet hung up and beamed at the phone. It was as though clouds had parted. She hadn't realised quite how badly she missed her family. Just knowing that her mum didn't hate her . . . oh, the relief. Without thinking, she touched the photo frame containing a picture of her and Tim. Tucked into the corner of it was a white feather.

Outside the window, she heard a car drive up and stop. A car door slammed. Someone hailed someone else. Harriet crossed the room and peered out. Tim was standing by his car, talking to Alice from the craft shop. He nodded as she talked animatedly to him. Harriet watched, smiling. Everyone in the village knew who he was now and they had accepted him, because they knew he was hers.

Still smiling, she cantered down the stairs and opened the door to the street. Both Tim and Alice looked up at the sound of the door unlatching. Alice waved and said, 'I'll leave you to get on, then.'

Tim grabbed his bag from the back of the car and crossed over to where Harriet was waiting. He came inside and, as the door clicked shut, they stepped into each other's arms. Where they belonged.

Acknowledgments

Belonging was inspired by Harriet herself. She showed up like a force of nature as a secondary character in *Snowed In* and just wouldn't leave my head. I wanted to find out about her, why did drink so much? Why was she so aggressive in her pursuit of Vinnie? I spent some time thinking about her and realised that she was grieving and trying not to think about it. While I was making notes one day, Niamh popped up and things evolved from there.

The Trewton Royd stories came about because I wrote a short story called 'Pat's Pantry' and, for some reason, I found that the voices in it were all from West Yorkshire. When I was a teenager, I lived in village in between Halifax and Huddersfield. It was far less rural than Trewton Royd, but probably as picturesque. For the first few weeks after I moved there, I couldn't understand a word anyone said, although they understood me perfectly. Once I 'got me ear in', I loved the Yorkshire accent.

I love Trewton Royd and these novellas are just my excuse for hanging out in the village.

Thanks: First of all, as always, thank you Jen Hicks, who sees all my stories before anyone else does and is an inspiration. Thank you to the fantastic ladies of the Naughty Kitchen for moral support, cake, advice, cake and making me laugh when I really need it. A special thanks to Kate Johnson who proofread the book for me and calmed my paranoia. Thank you Jane Eastgate, editor extraordinaire, for all of the notes.

As always, thank you to my husband and kids for putting up with my disappearing into my head from time to time. Special thanks to my daughter for feedback on covers.

★   ★   ★

Lastly, thank you to you, for buying this book so that I can afford to keep writing more.

We do hope that you have enjoyed reading this large print book.

Did you know that all of our titles are available for purchase?

We publish a wide range of high quality large print books including:
Romances, Mysteries, Classics
General Fiction
Non Fiction and Westerns

Special interest titles available in large print are:
The Little Oxford Dictionary
Music Book, Song Book
Hymn Book, Service Book

Also available from us courtesy of Oxford University Press:
Young Readers' Dictionary
(large print edition)
Young Readers' Thesaurus
(large print edition)

For further information or a free brochure, please contact us at:
Ulverscroft Large Print Books Ltd.,
The Green, Bradgate Road, Anstey,
Leicester, LE7 7FU, England.
Tel: (00 44) **0116 236 4325**
Fax: (00 44) **0116 234 0205**

Other titles in the
Linford Romance Library:

LOVE AND LIES

Jenny Worstall

When Rosie Peach arrives for her interview to become Shaston Convent School's new piano teacher, the first person she meets is striking music master David Hart. As her new role gets underway, Rosie comes up against several obstacles: her predecessor Miss Spiker's infamous temper, a bunch of unruly but loveable schoolgirls, and her swiftly growing feelings for David. The nuns of the convent are determined to meddle their way towards a school romance, but David is a complex character, and Rosie can't help but wonder what secrets he is hiding . . .

GAY DEFEAT

Denise Robins

Disarmingly lovely, Delia Beringham is the only daughter of a wealthy financier who indulges her every whim. It is Delia's hope that her lover, Lionel Hewes, will leave his wife for her — but the sudden crash of the Beringham family fortune and her father's suicide change all that. Lionel abruptly fades from the picture, and Delia is left with only her own courage and determination to sustain her. So what is she to say when her father's friend, Martin Revell, chivalrously offers her his hand in marriage?

LORD SAWSBURY SEEKS A BRIDE

Fenella J. Miller

If he is to protect his estate and save his sister from penury, Lord Simon Sawsbury must marry an heiress. Annabel Burgoyne has no desire to marry, but wishes to please her parents, who are offering a magnificent dowry in the hope of enticing an impecunious aristocrat. As Simon and Bella, along with their families, move to their Grosvenor Square residences for the Season, it's not long before the neighbours are drawn together. But when events go from bad to worse, will Simon sacrifice his reputation to marry Bella?

MURDER AT THE HIGHLAND PRACTICE

Jo Bartlett

Shortly after her return to the Scottish Highlands, DI Blair Hannah's small team of detectives is called upon to investigate a suspicious death in the rural town of Balloch Pass. The elderly woman had altered her will before she died, leaving everything to two unlikely beneficiaries: the local priest, and the town's new GP, Dr Noah Bradshaw. As Blair races against time to catch a potential killer, can she beat the ghosts of her past and grab the chance of her own happy ever after?

MACGREGOR'S COVE

June Davies

Running the Bell Inn, which sits high above Macgregor's Cove, is a busy yet peaceful life for Amaryllis's family — but their lodger Kit Chesterton arrives with a heavy secret in tow, which threatens to disturb the quiet waters. Meanwhile, a recent influx in contraband starts ripples of suspicion about smugglers, and Amaryllis's sister sets her sights on Adam Whitlock, who has recently returned from India with a shady companion. Despite the sinister events washing through the Cove, love surfaces as friendship becomes romance and strangers become family.